A SECRET LETTER TO A

*W*OMAN'S
*H*EART

A SECRET LETTER TO A

WOMAN'S HEART

DEBORAH BAIN

iUniverse, Inc.
Bloomington

A SECRET LETTER TO A WOMAN'S HEART

This is a work of fiction. All of the characters, names, incidents, organizations, and dialogue in this novel are either the products of the author's imagination or are used fictitiously.

iUniverse books may be ordered through booksellers or by contacting:

iUniverse
1663 Liberty Drive
Bloomington, IN 47403
www.iuniverse.com
1-800-Authors (1-800-288-4677)

ISBN: 978-1-4759-4161-6 (sc)
ISBN: 978-1-4759-4162-3 (ebk)

Printed in the United States of America

iUniverse rev. date: 08/15/2012

Mama for teaching me to always be true to myself, and Daddy for showing me how a man should be.

A SECRET LETTER TO A WOMAN'S HEART

I always thought that Grandma was weak because she always let people hurt her in ways that I never could. Grandma loved people in a way that I didn't understand. I didn't want to be like that. It was just too painful for anyone to bear. No human heart could handle it. That kind of pain kills and that's how grandma died. Loving people too much broke her heart. I didn't realize that when grandma decided to walk with the Lord, that people like her love in a different way, and even though, people hurt them badly, they can't do anything but love them. Only those who truly walk with the Lord can love like that. Grandma has been dead and gone twelve years and I'm just beginning to learn what that kind of love is, and what it really means.

In the eighteen years of my marriage to Raymond, I began to understand Grandma's kind of love for others. In my marriage, as in most, I found myself in situations that I preferred not to be in. I wanted to believe that no matter what, the situation Raymond and I would always do the right thing. We realized that if we made the wrong decision, we would cause each other pain and heartache.

My woman's instincts told me that other women would look at and desire my husband, and his instincts told him that men will look at and desire me. In all that I still hoped that my husband would love me enough and be faithful enough to remember that he is married to one woman. I never thought that he would break our marriage vows. I was a fool to think that our love would not let him do such an injustice to our marriage, but again I was wrong.

Raymond was not a GQ model, but he was good looking and sexy to me. Raymond was 6'2 with dark skin, soft and smooth to the touch. Just looking at him, said that he was a man who believed in taking care of his skin. He had put on weight, the kind that men develop around the waist, but that didn't matter to me, because when I looked at him I still saw that sexy hunk of a man, I fell in love with and married. I always loved to rub and kiss his lips, because they always reminded me of those chocolate kiss lips they sell for Valentine's Day. Each and every time I looked at him, my heart swelled with love, more love than I thought I was capable of feeling, let alone giving.

Raymond and I had gone through so many things in the eighteen years of our marriage. It had always been difficult from the start. His family especially his mother, didn't think that I was good enough for him. Neither of us had great finances, and I had two children going into this marriage. Oh boy! That was something that his mom really hated. She thought that I just wanted him because of his job. His mom claimed to be so spiritual minded, but not once, did she see that this was the will of God. His entire family saw was a woman with children looking for a man who would take care of her. They saw a woman who was taking him away from God and all the things that he was taught. No one saw the love that flowed between us. No one saw the way we looked at each other. It's funny that when people fall in love, they think that their love will conquer all. They seriously believe that love will bring them through. I never thought that he would be the one to help me to Christ. Well I was about to find out just how strong love and committed we were to our marriage and to each other.

The very thing I thought that he would not do, he did. I had just come back from visiting with my dying father. Raymond and I had never been away from each other for long periods of time either. Even though I sometimes had moments of doubt, I just never believed or just never wanted to believe that he would do something like that. It was nearing the end of the year, and so much was going on. We were about to purchase a home. I had left the Pentecostal church I was attending, and my husband had done the same. Now we were driving almost two hours to attend an AME Church pastured by Cody, Raymond's brother. That was different for us. The order of service was structured and sometimes stiff. Cody did not want it to be like that all the time, but with it being an AME church, those were their rules. Add my father's dying, to all of this. He was at the point where my stepmom had to do everything for him. She was a petite woman; short in stature and only about 119 pounds, but her action and power were that of a giant. I knew that she would need help and I wanted to, because that was my daddy. I wanted to look at him and just be near him even if he didn't know I was there.

My stepmother would help anybody, she would give until there was nothing left to give, but she could be forceful if the need arose. Even though she was a strong woman, seeing daddy lying in that bed day after day and dying slowly hurt her because she was not ready for him to leave her. He was her road dog. They did everything together.

They understood each other. They had something together that some people never find in their life time. She knew that she had been blessed. God blessed her with a good and faithful man, and now he was leaving her all alone. It was just as important for me to be there for him as it was for her.

At the same time that we were dealing with the purchase of a new home, changing church affiliation, supporting my stepmother and caring for my daddy, my mama was going through a painful time with her arm. She just had surgery. She needed to be taken care of. She was more than capable of taking care of herself, but mama really needed someone to be there even if she was very independent. Mama had always been this super woman to my sisters and me. She was a single parent raising three children. She worked two jobs just so we could have the things that we needed. Mama was a pretty woman. Mama could sing. It's funny how I grew up thinking that my mama was so mean and won't let me have fun in life, but when I grew up in the mind and not just the body, I realized that she was a smart cookie. Everything that she did or didn't do was for my good, and she loved and wanted what was best for me. Once I understood that I realized just how wonderful mama really is.

On my plate, also were our oldest son Maxwell and his wife Connie who were expecting baby number two. They were already in financial trouble, and with the new baby coming they were falling deeper in debt. Connie had been let go from her job. She was not able to do anything to contribute financially to help ease the burden. I knew that they would not be coming for Thanksgiving anymore. I don't think that Connie wanted to be near us, let alone spend any time with us. I knew that she didn't really care for us. I never understood why.

Then, I thought maybe it was because we didn't think that they should be getting married so soon. They had not known each other long and Maxwell needed to get some money together before starting a family.

Even with so much going on, we were able to continue to help with the finances. Being a parent and seeing the hard times they were having left us no choice but to help them. We prayed and hoped that God would answer our prayers and lighten the load for them. I knew it was best that I stay out of his life as much as possible. After they were married, Connie would always call him a mama's boy. I never liked hearing that because it didn't feel right. I didn't run his life nor did his father. We would tell him what we thought if he asked, but as far as interfering in his life we did not do. We raised both our boys, Maxwell and David, to be independent and responsible men. If Maxwell had been such the mama's boy that she had claimed him to be, then he would not have married her, at least not so soon.

Some in our home and others elsewhere, so there were all kinds of troubles going on, and I really did not need another one. I had all I felt I could handle, things got worse, with the exception of us now owning our home. Maxwell would not be coming back to spend Thanksgiving with us again because his wife does not want to come here anymore. What my heart longed for was what I call "the good old days." That time includes not only the eighteen years spent in a so called "perfect marriage" but also the four year courtship before.

Raymond had been a gentle man, always careful to make sure that I was happy, comfortable, secure, and satisfied in every way. Where did that Raymond go and when did he start to disappear? Raymond and I had never been away from one another for longer than a week at a time, but I had traveled home alone for a month here, a month there. I returned home in time for the holidays. Plus there was a lot of packing to do.

Thanksgiving and Christmas were nice with family and friends coming over. There was never any sign that our marriage was in trouble, other than that Thursday. I was in Atlanta, and we were talking and I told Raymond that I would be coming home on that Sunday instead of that Saturday. He became very upset and hung up the phone. I called him back and we had it out, and then I hung up. He called back about two hours later and told me I could stay and he would get an apartment for himself. He would pack up my stuff and I could get it when I got ready and go right back to Atlanta. I told him, whatever Raymond.

"I don't know why you are acting so crazy."

"I'm not acting crazy. You are the one who doesn't want to come home."

"Raymond it is not that I don't want to come home. I just want to see daddy for a little longer."

"Kathy you have been gone for a month. I want you home."

"Okay Raymond I will be home on schedule."

Even with that one incident I never would have believed that something was so wrong that Raymond would do what he had done. We spent our New Years Eve moving into our new home. I thought this finally was our beginning to be able to settle down. No more moving from this place to that. Looking forward to being happy and creating memories here. This new start should have been one of the happiest times of our lives. Material things can never give you what the heart longs for. We were in the home for only two days. I was never one for being patient, so before Raymond could get back to the house I had taken it upon myself to hang the drapes. Raymond didn't want the ones that we had in the living room. He thought that they were not long enough. I, on the other hand, thought that they would do just fine. When that man gets it into his head how he wants something there is no changing his mind, so I took down the drapes and left the house.

Raymond was angry because I had left home without saying where I was going. To make him even angrier, I left my phone because I didn't want to talk with him at the time. When I returned home, it was about 9:30 at night, and he was planning to leave the house. I wanted to know where he was going.

"I'm not going anywhere. I was just messing with you, because you left the house," he said in a sarcastic tone.

"Why would you want to do something like that?" I asked.

"Cause we seem to be getting on each other's nerve. I don't know if I can make you happy anymore. I don't know if I want to do this any longer," he explained.

"Well Raymond why did we buy a house if you are having all of these doubts?"

"Because no matter what happens, we still need a place to stay, and I have to take care of you. I remember when we first got married. We talked about our future, how you were going to have your own restaurant or become a news journalist. What the hell happen? I feel as if it were not for me that you would have done those things. You seem to have lost your drive," he was almost sad.

Why couldn't being a wife and mother be enough for me? Why couldn't the things that I have done, be enough. What if they were the most important things in my life? I could feel the tears falling and I tried to stop them, but they just kept coming, so I just gave up and let them fall as hard as they wanted to come. All my life I felt as if I had been thrown away and all I ever wanted was to be loved, truly loved by my man and my family. And the one thing that I wanted most in life seems to be the one thing that I couldn't have. Don't get me wrong. It's good to have nice homes, cars and other material things, but the most important thing to me is the love.

Raymond walked up behind me and wrapped his arms around me and I walked off with a deep cry in my throat. I walked into the bathroom to try and gain some type of control of myself so that I could continue the conversation. Our bedroom exits into an open area between the formal living and dining room. Just beyond that area is the foyer with two large glass doors that allows a view of the front yard. In the dining room are three windows that I walked over to and stood in front of. I looked onto the screened in patio and watching the water shoot up out of the fountain in the pool. Raymond was right there where I left him. I had always been gifted with the ability to have dreams that brought meaning or focus to actual events. Once, during a hospital stay, I had dreamed a conversation between Raymond and his sister-in-law Linda. For just a few minutes he held me as if he wanted to remember what it felt like. I could almost sense that he felt that he would not hold me like this ever again. As I continued to look out of the window, I told him that, I must have fallen off to sleep while setting in the car; I could hear him and a woman talking in my sleep. It reminded of the dream I had when I was asleep and I could hear you and Linda talking about me. When I woke up I could tell you everything that you and the other woman talked about.

"Did you hear what we said?" he asked hesitantly.

"No and yes, and I don't think I want to know." I could not bring myself to ask the question that was in the back of my mind, so I didn't. We went about the rest of the evening avoiding what we both knew was coming next. We went to bed with so much unsaid. I could not get any sleep. So the next morning I had to ask Raymond.

"Raymond did you sleep with her? He just looked at me and sighed, I'm waiting and I want an answer, Raymond!"

"Yes Kathy, I slept with her."

All I could do was run out of the room and holler and cry to the top of my voice, but the tears would not come. I needed them to come so some of the pain would go away. But they wouldn't. They wouldn't give me the relief that I so desperately needed, so I went back into the bedroom to find that he had gone into the bathroom and locked the door.

Beating on the door of the bathroom, I screamed, "Open the mother fucking door. Open the door, Raymond!"

Raymond opened the door with his toothbrush in his mouth, but when he opened the door he backed away as if I was about to jump him. When he finished brushing his teeth, he came and sat on the bed. I stood in front of the sliding glass door.

"How many times did you sleep with her?" He just looked as if I had not said a word. "Answer my got-damn question!" I continued screaming.

"I slept with her twice, Kathy, only twice," Raymond confessed.

"Only twice!" Is that supposed to mean something? Well it doesn't mean shit. You broke your vows to me and to God. I don't understand why. What was it? Is she pretty, fine? Does she look better than me? Was her pussy tighter? What the fuck was it, Raymond?

He yelled at me, "It was not about you. It was not because of anything that you did. It's me that's fucked up."

"I must have done something, because you hurt me. You broke my heart, you motherfucker. You tore my whole life apart. You know what you need to do. Go see a lawyer and file for a divorce."

"I'm not doing a thing, and I'm not leaving and going anywhere," he yelled.

"Oh yes the fuck you are," I almost laughed. "You're doing something because if you think you are going to screw me and her you've lost your damn mind. Raymond, did she give you head too?"

I walked to the dresser and ran my arm across it and everything came flying off. Nothing but rage and anger, pain and longing, love and wanting, too damn much for anyone person to feel at one time.

"Well I tell you one thing, I'm not going anywhere and if you want to fuck that bitch, then you go ahead because you will not be fucking me. Hell if I get that desperate I can get a toy for my own pleasures, because I am not yet dead. And let her know that she will never get up in here, because I ain't going anywhere, and you can't keep taking care of me and her so go ahead and fuck if you want to, you are doing it any damn way."

I continued to stand at the sliding glass door. I looked out watching the fountain in the pool. I think I was saying this more to myself than to him. I first thought that no one would want me, and then I thought why they wouldn't. If they want Raymond, why not me. I may not have a great job, but I'm a great catch, and who knows one day I will be big in name and people will know me all over for the good I do and not the bad.

I spent the next two days wishing and wanting this not to be true and wanting the pain to stop. I was not able to think of anything else. I could not begin to tell anyone how I lived through those two days. I did not want to believe that this was really happening to me. I waited for Raymond to tell me that everything was going to be alright and that we would get counseling and fix our marriage.

Raymond worked long hours on his job. It would always be dark when he reached home. I would always have his dinner ready. He would come in, put his lunch box down, and head for the office. From the kitchen, I could see him at work while I prepared his food. When the food was ready, Raymond sat at the table we had in the breakfast nook. It was a dark chocolate oval shaped table that sat in front of three windows, like the ones in the dining room. I sat across from him. I needed answers, and I knew that because he was not saying anything. I knew I had to ask. Did he love her? Did he want to be with her? The only thing he told me was that he didn't know.

I knew then that he had answered my question because if he loved me enough he would have said that he wanted to work on us without any more women, and that he wanted me one day to trust him again, but those words never came out of his mouth.

Then I thought about my grandma. What would she say about this mess? I knew she would still find a way to tell me that if I still loved him that we would make it through this. Only this time, I didn't know if grandmamma would be right. All I could do was get up from the table, because all the emotions came flooding in and they overwhelmed me. I ran a bubble bath. I lit the candles and closed myself in the bathroom. Once I got into the tub, all I could do was cry. After all the emotions that were flowing within me died down, the love was still there. I still loved the way he makes me feel when he touches me. I still wanted him because I truly love him with everything that is in me. I still want to make love to him. I still want to get old with him and see the world together. What does a woman do when her man no longer wants that with her? It's crazy what the mind does to a woman when a man cheats on her.

After my bath, I had to go back out and look at him, all the while remembering what he said to me. I stayed out there long enough to clean the kitchen and make sure that I put his drinks in the freezer for the next day. When I finished I went to bed. I wondered if he was going to see her tonight, or had he just come from her house. Would he see her tomorrow? So many different emotions! So many emotions to go through. I just cradled in my bed and prayed that sleep would over take me. I needed peace and sleep was the only way I could think to get it.

Tuesday morning when I awoke, I did not remember or feel the pain, but that did not last long. The harsh reality of a marriage gone bad came back with a hurricane effect. Raymond was off today and I had no idea what was going to happen. So I washed up, went into the kitchen to busy myself. When I looked up and saw Raymond coming from the bedroom, dressed with his keys in his hand, I could feel the tears in the back of my eyes, but I did not want him to see them. I looked at the clock on the stove. It was 11:45. Raymond walked around the counter, stood beside me and gave me a kiss that made my feet tingle. He had not kissed me like that in a long time, or maybe I just hadn't felt that way in a long time. When he walked out that door, all that I had just felt was replaced with all the pain and fear that a body could consume.

Time moved as if it had been put into slow motion. It is now 3:36 p.m. and he wasn't yet back. I couldn't help wondering what he was doing. I tried to stay busy and to keep my mind from wondering. I knew that I had to forgive him and I think I already had because I wanted him just that bad and I wanted us to work. I needed it to work. He was my life and I didn't know how to live my life without him in it. I did know that I would never forget just how he hurt me. No one could have hurt me as deeply as Raymond had. How was I going to keep it from the boys? Could I find strength to act as if life is good? I didn't know, but I knew that I would soon find out. David had not been home for the last couple of days. This worked out for me because I did not want to explain to him what was going on between his father and me. It is so funny that I would be thinking of David because when he walked through that door I had to be the best actor I could be.

David walked over to me and gave me a kiss on the forehead, "Ha mama, how are you doing?"

"I'm doing well now that I see you."

"Where is daddy?"

"I don't know. He left this morning and hasn't returned yet."

"Well speaking of the devil," David said as Raymond walked through the door.

"What's up nigger?"

"You the nigger, nigger," replied David.

All I could do was watch the display of love and affection between a father and a son. If he knew what his dad had done, it would rock the very foundation that he believed in. I had to be strong for the children. I couldn't let our life be a lie. I had to keep it together. I tried to protect others but who the hell was there to protect me? I wanted to pray. I needed to pray, but I didn't know what to say. I understood what God meant when he said love would cover a multitude of sin. He was right again. Love doesn't go anywhere. Sometimes the pain can over shadow it, but it always raises its head. David stayed at the house long enough to get a bath and grab something to eat.

"Ma, I'll be home on the weekend?"

"Okay, I guess you like this girl."

"Ya, I think I do, but you know I have to be careful, cause girls get crazy, man."

"That's what happens when you just love them and leave."

I just looked at Raymond. How the hell would he know? Oh yeah, I forgot he's the Mac daddy now. It took everything in me to keep from crying. When David did leave I had only enough energy to get into bed and sleep. At least I could leave all of this drama and pain for awhile. When Raymond came to bed and touched me, I just turned to water in his arms. He would make love to me and my world would be okay, until morning. I guess I was looking for hope in the sex. I wanted to find something that had long been gone out of our relationship.

Dealing with our situation when I was awake was hard, but it had haunted my sleep at night now. I could not find a peaceful moment in my life and it began to take its toll on me. I began to notice different smells on Raymond when he came home. Sometimes it would be smoke and at other times it would be a mixer of other things. I could only believe that it was the smell of the other woman. I remember when I used to smoke and Raymond acted as if the smoke would kill him. Now all he smells like is smoke.

When Raymond and I were first married we did everything together, but when the conflicts with his family became more intense, I think that is when the separation began. Thinking back the separation could have started when the Lord told me to go to this other church, because I needed to grow quickly in order to be in the place I needed to be when he raised Raymond up to do his will. Then even with that I was met with opposition. Whatever happen to trying the spirit by the spirit to see if it be of God, but then why do that? God could not have possibly told me to do anything, since I was not worthy to be Raymond's wife in the first place. He use to take me with him when he went out, but now he doesn't want me along and if I ask him to do something he always seems to forget to do it. I and the things that concerned our life were becoming unimportant. I could not help paying attention to every little thing now. When he did get home, the drama and the emotions that I dealt with while he was gone would meet him at the door. There would be another blow-up and I'd cry. We always found a civil ground to go back to once we reached that plateau. Then we would talk and go on as if life was fine with us. I would make his plate and give him something to drink. I would set it in front of him and he would continue with his endearing remarks.

If we didn't act like two crazy people, then I don't know what. After a blow-up like that I would always run a bubble bath, light the candles and just soak. I even began to drink more wine. I went from one glass twice a week to a glass every day. When Raymond would finish eating or whatever he was doing, he would come and get in the tub with me. I would never tell him that he couldn't or that I didn't want him to because he knew I did. These scenes began to take over our lives. The moments became days, and the days became weeks. It was sickening even to me. I could not control or help myself. As much as I hated that

I still wanted him to touch me, knowing that he probably just got through touching her, I still wanted Raymond to make love to me. I knew that after that bath we would make love. I knew that Raymond would touch me in that water, that his hand would find its way to the most sensitive spot on my body. I antiapated his touch. I longed for it, and I couldn't wait for him to show me that he still desired and needed me.

I use to see other women in my situation and think now how screwed-up is that? Well, now I know just how fucked-up it really is. Now I know what made Grandma stay with Granddaddy. It had been about the love and nothing else. No security or anything would make a woman continue to stay and love a man knowing that he is not faithful to her. It had been a month now and the roller coaster ride of emotions was still going on. I had not been to church since I became aware of my husband's infidelity. I did not know why but I felt the need to go to church, so I called my friend Barbara to find out what time church started. I really needed the Lord to speak to me, my heart, just speak. Barbara and I didn't talk all the time, so when she answered the phone I expected the sarcasm.

"Well, well what do I owe the honor of this call?'

"I know right."

How are you doing?

"I'm fine, just calling to find out what time does church start."

"It starts at 11:00, but I wasn't planning on going to church today."

"That's okay, I just felt like going and I thought why not go to your church. It's down the road and I have not been in a long time.'

"Well since you are coming, it would only be right for me to meet you there."

"Barbara, you don't have to come. It will be good to see you, but I can go to the house and visit."

"You and Raymond can come anyway." Michael cooked dinner. The two of you can join us."

"Ok then see you at church." Walking out the bathroom.

Raymond was still in the bedroom and I told him about my plans to go to Barbara's church and then to their house. I asked him if he needed me to do something for him before I left, but he told me that he would be going with me.

I thought that was interesting; nevertheless, I was glad that he would be with me, so I wouldn't be wondering if he was home or with her. We went to our friend's church. Service was really nice and I enjoyed myself because Raymond was there with me. After church, we told Barbara and Michael that we would come over for dinner as soon as we went back to the house because we were to meet the yard man. We made it to Michael and Barbara's had dinner, good conversation, and good company. The entire day had been so wonderful. I could not have asked for a more perfect day than that.

When we arrived home, Raymond told me that he was going to a business class. It was being held at Ms. Carrie's church. He wanted to get really serious about his business and he wanted to see if he could get the kind of help he needed. I was okay, and yet not okay, because I didn't know if he was telling the truth or if he was lying so he could see her. I started to realize that when he had vacation time or was off, he would tell me at the last minute, because he had already made plans to be with her and not with me. Even when I went to attend to my father, he could have come but she was more important than I. So when he left all of the emotions began to stir and my stomach got knots in it. As the hours passed, the emotions got more intense, until I had to get in my car and leave the house.

No longer could I stand being alone and let my mind do what it was doing. I turned on the radio and began to listen to the *quiet storm*, where the D. J. played all the music lovers wanted to hear while making love. Then the tears came. I began to scream and yell to the top of my lungs. I had to stop for a moment because I seemed crazy even to myself crying and screaming like a mad woman. But I was beyond even my control. There seem to be no helping myself. No way to control the pain. No way to get it to listen to me, the side that through it all still had some reasoning. So then, I prayed.

"Oh God, Oh God, why did this have to happen to me? All I wanted was for him to love me forever, and he couldn't even do that. What did I do that was so wrong that he would hurt me this badly? If it was not a sin to kill myself I would gladly do it just to stop the pain. Please God take the pain away, please? I can't take it anymore."

Instead of going straight home I rode a little longer, still not ready to go home. The sane part of me begins to come back, to calm down, and to breathe easy. As those things began to happen I realized that I did not want Raymond to know that I was so out of it that I left the house. It was as if I wanted him to know my pain, but not see just how bad it was affecting me. Again, I was like some insane woman I knew. The ride was not doing what I needed it to do, because then I started to look for him, and the more I looked the sicker I became in my stomach. When I thought I couldn't take anymore I got a text from Raymond.

"Still *at meeting, this turned out to be church. Will see you when over.*"

"Okay, I'll see you when I see you."

Pretending to be nonchalant, I knew damn well what he was doing. That just brought me back to myself. Now I can take my black ass home and wait for my baby. I had just closed the garage door and walked into our bedroom when I heard the alarm announce garage door open."

"Ha where are you just coming from?"

"I had to go for a ride. I started to feel closed in, and my mind began to go all over the place." I walked right into his arms, and laid my head on his chest. It felt so good there. The world was alright with me as long as we stayed like that.

"I did something and I need you to stand and believe with me."

"What did you do?"

"I pledged a $1000.00 and I believe that God is going to do this and I need you to be with me on this."

"If you exercised faith no matter what kind in the state-of-mind that you are in, hell ya! I will stand with you." Love was made that night, too. Too much thinking is never good for anyone. I couldn't go to sleep, so I started thinking about what he had asked of me. It's not so funny when a man can come and ask you to stand by his side, but he can't even stand by his marriage. It makes you wonder out of the two who is the bigger fool, and yet here we are to do battle another day.

"Raymond don't forget that you have to see Dr. Carr at 10:45 this morning."

"I remember and I have also to get blood drawn."

I didn't even ask him if he wanted me to tag along because he would usually ask me to come or tell me to let's go. I wanted him to ask me to go so badly, but when he didn't my heart took another nose dive into the pain that was there. The whole got a little deeper and a little wider. It felt like he was telling me with everything that he did just how much he didn't want me or our marriage. So he left without me, I got dressed and drove to Orlando, so I could go to Burlington Coat Factory and spend my gift card, but first I had to stop by Stephanie, my sister-in-law and tell her what has happened.

"Hello Kathy, what are you doing on this side of town? Are you going to the meat store?"

"No, I am going to Burlington's. My cousin gave me a card for Christmas."

"Oh, if you don't mind I would like to ride with you. I don't have anything to do."

"I would enjoy the company and I need to tell you what is going on."

"Please don't tell me bad news."

"I don't want to tell anyone, but I have to talk to someone, and you are that person. Raymond has been cheating on me."

"Oh no, Kathy! Please tell me that you are joking.'

"That's not something you joke about."

"I can't believe it. 'Not Raymond. No not him."

"Yes him! I didn't want to believe it either, but it is what it is." Just then my cell phone rang. That was David.

"Yes baby what's up?"

"Mama, where are you?"

"I'm in Orlando. Why? What do you want?"

"I have to be at work at 1:00 today."

"Call your dad and see if he has left the doctor's office, and ask him to take you to work."

"Okay. Bye Mama, love ya."

"Okay. Where was I? Oh, we had a big blow-up and it all came out, and a lot of things were said. I don't know what I'm going to do."

The phone rang again.

"Mama, daddy won't pick-up."

"Okay, I will try to reach him, and if I can't I will drive back and take you to work, okay.'

"Thanks Mama, bye."

"Stephanie, let me try and reach Raymond because I really don't want to have to go back home. If I have to go back I know that I will not be back over this way today."

"I'll drive you back and then you won't have to worry about gas."

"No you don't need to do that. I will have to come another time." I started back because Raymond didn't answer his phone so I had to go back. By the time I got about twelve miles from home Raymond called.

"Hello."

"Ha babe, I have David."

"Okay, so how did your appointment go?"

"Not good."

"What's up?"

"My blood pressure was too high, my sugar level is really high and I need to get blood work and get an x-ray of my hand and wrist."

"Okay so we just have to do some things and everything will be fine okay."

"I hear ya."

"Well, since you hear me, ask David where my house key is?"

"He said that he has it."

"Well I can't get into the house."

"I will get one made and I'll drop it off on my way back."

"Is it okay if I go with you?"

"Sure I will be there in about twenty minutes."

"I'll be waiting." I pulled into the drive way and I waited. I checked myself to make sure that Raymond liked what he saw when he pulled up.

"Mmm, don't we look good? Your jeans cuffed with your boots on. Your hair in a ponytail looking real good."

"Why thank you, Mr. Scott."

"You are quite welcome, Mrs. Scott."

I remember feeling as we began backing out of the drive way how strange it felt riding in the car with him because now I knew that she had been in my seat, and they may have held hands while driving. That was once special for us, but I didn't know if it was anymore. Did he open the door for her like he did for me? Everything that had once been about him and me was now about her too. I tried to focus on positive things because I didn't want to cry, but not in front of Raymond. I don't know if I wanted to be strong for him, because I didn't want him regretting that he let me come, or that I needed to pretend that all was well in our life. For whatever the reason, I had to give my stellar performance and that I did.

In the midst of all that, the day turned out to be a very good day. We went home and he helped me cook dinner. I thought that was just the sweetest thing. I dreamed last night that Raymond had taken me to this woman's house and thought it was a friend, a friend she was indeed. She let me know how it was with the two of them and what he didn't need from me. She could take care of him better than I could. I don't know why I dreamed like that. We made love last night and it was very different and really intense, until I felt the scratches on his back. Then I started to think of her lying underneath him. I imagined how she felt when he was in her. I also wondered why he never got on top of me so that I could feel that way to the point that I would want to scratch in his back. It was like the mind being rewind with old movies. These things I thought about and then just pushed away.

I was so glad that David had moved in with that girl. We didn't know her name or what she looked like. One thing for sure, whoever she was David really took a liking to her. For him to have moved in with her, we knew this was a serious relationship for him. It was as if God knew that we needed that time alone and that the boys did not need to know just yet. I still did not know what I was going to do. I knew what I wanted, but it would not work without Raymond's participation, so everything was still in the air.

I was standing in the kitchen at the sink when he came up behind me and began to kiss me and suck on my neck, invoking feelings that traveled all over my body. It's the kind that lovers feel in the beginning of a relationship, the kind that make them have eyes only just for each other. I could feel his manhood hardening and he whispered a promise of love making when he returned, and that is when it all came crashing down. Was he now going to see her? Why did he have to leave me now? Would he make love to her and would he be too tired to love me as he promised. As he walked out the door, I couldn't help looking after him, with a look of loss and longing in my eyes. I didn't think that he would turn around and see, but he did ask me what was wrong.

I said, "Nothing Raymond."

"I know maybe not with your mouth, but with your eyes you spoke volumes."

I walked out of sight thinking that he would just go and leave me to my pain, but he came in and watched me.

I turned and said, "I thought that you were gone."

Raymond just stood looking. Then he turned and walked out. Before he looked away, I saw his pain, but I was hurting too badly to even reach out to him. I didn't want to think anymore so I busied myself with things to keep my mind off of him and her.

Four hours passed. It was time for dinner and Raymond had not returned. What was he doing this time of night? It was driving me crazy! Then I heard the garage door open and I felt my nerves jumping all over the place. I kept telling myself that I would not ask Raymond where he had been. I would act as if I did not care and that his being gone for four hours did not bother me. But when he walked through that door everything I said I wouldn't do went out the window.

"So where have you been? I guess you just had to see her. You couldn't wait to get away from me so you could fuck her."

"No, Kathy, that is not what, happened. I had every intention of being gone for only half an hour, but when I saw that pain in your eyes and on your face, I just couldn't come right back and face you, knowing that I was the one that caused it."

"So you thought staying away from home was the best darn solution? Well we can tell that was very bright of you. It's so funny how you never really thought about all this before you did it, because all this shit about you facing me and my pain is just that, shit." I just walked out of the kitchen. I didn't want to hear anymore of Raymond's lies. I had already had one glass of wine that gave me a reason to get another. At least I would sleep tonight.

For the next couple of days things were okay. I was able to hold my emotions in check at least enough to feel as if my life had some sort of normalcy to it. It would always take something to trigger the storm that was waiting to be unleashed. Only when it came out there was no controlling it. All the things that I should remember and fall back on in the bible do not mean a thing. All I can see and feel is the pain that I have. I somehow forget that I am suppose to be a child of God. I know God, I think of God until that storm comes and what was done.

Today was a good day until I found a condom in Raymond's work pants and all the emotions started again. How many nights did he tell me he was at work and he went to her house for a quickie, then, he came home to me and acted as if he had just left work and he was beat? He was beat from making love to her. Each day there seemed to be more. When would he tell me the whole truth? He was one sick mother fucker to do this, and each time it gets worst. All that shit he talked about last night was just that, shit. He just wanted to have his cake and eat it too.

When he walked in I said hello and fixed his plate and he sat down to eat. I then threw the condom on the table and told him that my day was going well until I found this in his work pants.

"So I guess you were going by her house to fuck before you came home!"

"No Kathy, that's the condom you found in my lunch box."

"You're a got damn lie because that condom is in the drawer in the bathroom, so that is not the same one."

Even though I was talking to Raymond in such a vile manner and knew that was not the way I should be talking,

I kept on speaking. With every word that I spoke, I wished Raymond pain, the same pain that he had caused me.

"Yes it is" he said, I put it in my pocket."

"No I think that you are confused, because I took it out and let it sit on the kitchen table for a whole week, to see if you would get it but you didn't."

"Well I'm not going to argue with you."

"Don't because it's a lie and you told it."

Even that should have told him just how dumb he was. Why would you even put a condom in your pants, when you should be going to work and coming home. He was saying without saying that he had every intention of going to fuck her again. There was no love making that night. He slept on his side of the bed and I slept on mine. We did not touch each other through the night. Getting that down time from any situation will make things seem not so bad, even if only for a little while.

Wednesday morning when the alarm clock went off, we both got up and moved doing what we always did. I prepared his breakfast and lunch and when he was ready, he kissed me and left. When Raymond got home from work I fed him and after that we headed out the door. While we were walking I said, "A penny for your thoughts." He told me that he did not have anything on his mind, so I looked away, because at that very moment I realized that I didn't know him, and I didn't even know what to say to him. He must have seen the look before I could turn because he then started to walk into me. "What are you doing?" I began to laugh. He smiled and showed me his teeth. That made me feel a little better. It was like I was willing to take whatever little attention he was willing to give because I was not ready to do without it so completely. Whatever crumb he threw I gladly took.

When we finished our walk, he took his bath and went to bed. I was left up again with my thoughts and all the fears that go with them. When I went to bed that night I could not sleep so I went into the family room and sat in the recliner, and I began to talk to the Lord.

Again I asked him why? What did I do, for this to happen to me? Eventually, I fell off to sleep.

"Kathy you need to come to bed. Why are you in here?"

"I couldn't sleep and didn't even know I had fallen sleep."

He was rubbing my forehead and it felt good, so I followed him to bed, and when he got in he turned his back to me and went right back to sleep. There was no holding me in his arms. There was no kissing my head, eyes, or my lips. So, I too turned my back to him and tried to go back to sleep. The alarm clock went off and I got up because I wasn't sleeping anyway. I went into the kitchen to get Raymond's lunch and breakfast ready. When he was ready to go, I walked out with him so that I could get the mileage. I had to keep up with that for his job. He gave me a kiss that had no feeling or meaning to it.

I kept telling myself that I was going to have a good day. I was going to make myself beautiful and think only positive thoughts. That day was not so bad. I don't know why or how. I only knew that it was more peace then I had in a long time. It worked until darkness began to fall. I became anxious and I wanted to get out, so I texted David to ask him for some gas money. He told me that he was not coming home, but I could come up to his job and get $25.00. He told me that he would be off at 7:00 p.m., so about 6:40 I headed that way. I got there a little early so I decided to call Raymond and find out how much longer he would be at work. He didn't answer so I hung up. Then I received a text from him.

"Right in the middle of something, will call u back in 10 minutes. What's up?"

So I texted back, "Nothing." I waited for his call and when 25 minutes had passed I figured that I would go by his job just to see if he was there. When I got there I didn't see his car, and my mind went straight to left field.

"Raymond where are you?" No sound at all. "Raymond where are you damn it!"

"Kathy, what the hell!"

"You motherfucker,' I screamed. 'You're with that bitch aren't you? You better not come home, bitch. I am going to kill you. You hear me? Don't you come home!" I hung up on him. I then called my stepmother and asked her to talk to me. Interrupting us, Raymond called me repeatedly. I wouldn't answer, because there was nothing to talk about. Because Raymond just wouldn't stop, I asked her to hold on.

"What Raymond! What the fuck do you want?"

"Kathy where are you?"

"That's what you fucking called me for," I hung up on him.

"Mama I have to go. I got things to do and I can't talk anymore."

"Kathy please don't do anything crazy!"

"Oh it's too late for that. He started this and I'm going to finish this."

I couldn't get to the house fast enough. I don't even remember driving home. All I knew was that my mind was racing so fast that I could not keep up with it. I couldn't stop what I was doing. I felt driven by something that I allowed to come in and take over. Once I was inside the house, I got a suitcase and just began to throw his shit in it.

I made sure I put his condoms in, too, because I was sure that he would need them. When I finished, I closed it and set it in front of the garage door.

I turned off all the lights and stood with the knife in my hand. I was going to kill him. That was the only way to stop the pain. I had to kill what caused it. He said that he wanted to work on our marriage and told all those lies. But he didn't mean them; he just wanted me to believe that shit so he could continue to do what he was doing. He didn't know that I knew what he had been telling his niece. He enjoyed what he was doing and he was not about to stop. Now I was going to help him stop. I patiently waited, and when I saw the car pull into the driveway, I positioned myself and stood ready, but that bastard did not come in the door he usually comes in.

He came in through the front door, calling my name. He wanted to know where I was. I was still in that position breathing like a raging bull. I was possessed by something that I did not want to fight. All I knew was that Raymond lied and was still lying and I just couldn't take it anymore. If I could not have him and he was my husband, then that bitch and no other bitch would have him.

He stood at the other side of the bar.

"What did I tell you?" he asked.

I just looked at him still breathing hard.

"What did I tell you I had to do today?"

"What! What you had to do today."

"Yes I told you I had to get a cash advance, so I could pay some bills. I couldn't even do it. You can't call and do that screaming and yelling like that. You can't act like that every time I go somewhere."

"Well, you should have thought about that before you went and did what you did."

"Kathy, I know. Don't you think that if I could go back and change things I would? If I could take away the pain that I have caused you I would. But I can't, and I don't know what to do?

"So, Raymond, what the fuck is that supposed to do for me? I want this to stop! I want my life back! I want my marriage back! I want to trust you again! I want to believe in you! I want to know that I can see you leave and not worry where you are or what you are doing!"

"So what's this you are leaving?"

"Hell no, you are!" I could hear the tears in his voice.

"So Kathy, where am I supposed to go?"

"I figured since you went to fuck her you could take your got damn ass back and stay with her."

"Oh so you are just going to put me out on the street. Just like that."

"No, Raymond not just like that. You think I want you to leave? Do you think I want to push you into the arms of another woman? Hell no! But I forgot your bitch ass already did that. I know we can't keep going on like this. You said that you have not seen her in a while, but that you like talking to her. So if you are still talking to her, then it is only a matter of time before you start fucking her again."

"No, that is not true."

"Yes, it is. You also said that you don't know what you are going to do. That you could not tell me what I needed or wanted to hear. So you are saying that this marriage is over."

"No, that is not what I am saying! See there you go not listening to me again. You don't pay attention to what I'm saying."

"Okay Raymond, then you tell me what is it you are saying."

"I'm saying that," he stopped and just looked at me, "I guess you are right."

Then there was nothing else to talk or fuss about because that was it. My head got it and understood what he had said, but my heart was still behind. We didn't talk anymore that night. I feed him, cleaned the kitchen, took a bath and went to bed. That night he held me, because I think we both knew that this would be the last time for us. Lying in his arms didn't feel like it was over, but I could not be a fool to what he had said. As much as I wanted him to change his mind I knew that he wouldn't. There was almost a calm about us, yet there was something brewing. Even though grandma knew that I had a temper, she would be very disappointed in my behavior. She always told me that a lady did not carry on in such a manner. The problem was I didn't feel much like being a lady.

The alarm clock woke me at 12:45 a.m. I did not want to get out of bed because I knew that if I did I would have to start again. Another day with the same problem pain that I didn't feel while I slept. As usual, I got Raymond's lunch ready and fixed his breakfast. I always walked him out to his car, because that is what he liked me to do.

As I closed the garage door, I knew that I was going to have a bad day and I wanted to call my sister-in-law, but I knew not to call at 2:30 in the morning. I felt as if I was about to break down, and I would not be able to help myself. All I could do was try to go back to sleep. That was the only way to suppress this madness that was trying to take hold of me. I slept on and off for the next four hours and when I woke up I refused to sleep anymore I washed up and decided it was time for me to have a talk with Jesus. I sat on the bed and just let go:

Well Lord, I guess this is really over, I can't do this anymore. I can't, go through what I went through last night. I was in such a rage, I really could have hurt him, had he not come in the way he did. I guess that sealed it all, because I can't live like this anymore. He doesn't want to change. He wants to do the things that he wants to do and I can't stop him. Yes we talked about it, but I didn't think. I really was hoping and praying that our love, his love for me, his love for you would sustain him, you know. That it would really keep him, but it didn't do that. It just didn't do that. He went anyway. He went because of the drive, the need, the urge to have an affair with another woman. His urge to party, to club, to do all of those things were far greater than his love for you or me. It's got to be his love for you that would keep him, or it has to be something that you put in us when you created us. You know. I guess he just doesn't have it. He says he loves me and I love him too, but I can't live like this anymore.

I don't want to iron his clothes and find another condom in his pocket. I don't want to be fixing his lunch and find a condom in his lunchbox. I don't want to wonder where he is, or if he is still at work, or has he gone to visit her on his lunch break, you know. I don't want to wonder about what he is doing on his days off because he doesn't want me to be with him. I just, I don't want to do all of this anymore God. I don't want to do it anymore, and I know (I almost laughed) you, that you. I can't even say it, cause every time I say you bless me with something or you did something looks like the enemy just comes in and he just takes over and wreaks havoc. It makes me wonder if I know what the hell I'm really talking about. I don't even know what I'm talking about when it comes to what you did or you are doing. Because I don't understand why you would go ahead and bless us with this home. My life is mucked the hell up, just mucked up, and I don't get it, I don't understand your *reasoning or your purpose for allowing this. I can't stay here, I'm not going to be able to live here and we are not together. I'm not going to be able to do it. I don't want to do it.*

I don't want to have to swallow my pride or humble myself to the existing of shame and embassasment, and degrading. I already feel like I am unworthy, that I wasn't enough, that I couldn't do or be all that I needed or could have been for him, I just can't do it anymore. In a way I guess I have nobody but myself to blame, because he, like I said we talked about where his flesh was, he was feeling. I just didn't think that it was going to be like this you know. I don't know what the hell I was thinking. I guess I wasn't thinking. Because if I was thinking, then you know what Lord, he's right then we wouldn't have gotten married. We wouldn't have gotten married, and he would have gone his way and I would have gone mine, and so much for that. I mean what are we suppose to do keep living in the house together, because we are eventually going to have to sleep in separate bedrooms, because I'm mmm going to tell you again that this is not working. He is too close and I haven't stop loving him. I still want to make love to him. But when I do, I think about him and her. How was it for her? What were they doing? How did she make him feel? Who wants to keep thinking like that? Who wants to feel like that? I know I don't! So God it has got to be something better. I can't say, because he isn't a bad man, he just has issues like the rest of us, you know. He's not a bad man, and any woman would be glad to have him, be blessed to have him once he gets his issues and stuff intact.

I just hate that we have put in nineteen years and its all for naught. Everything just went completely down the drain and for what you know. Why can't he to go out to a club or supper club with me. Why we can't go dancing? Why we can't do it together. But that is not what he wants. He doesn't want me.

He wants to do all of those things with other women, and then he wants to come home and to know that I'm here, because I'm going to cook, clean, wash and iron his clothes, and if by chance he succeeds he wants some not-not then I'll be the one that will be right here to give it to him you know, until he go out and meet up with somebody else or he get with the one that he is going to be messing with anyway. I can't do this; I can't live here like that, now I'll be a fool to be here and doing his cooking cleaning and this nigger running around. No, no, we have to establish some kind of ground rules here. I think that once we find rules that will be beneficial to the both of us; we can proceed with the divorce. Then I will leave, because I'm going to be the one that leaves. I'm not staying here in this house. I thank you for it Lord, but I ain't staying here. When I leave he can have all the women he wants and I wish him all the best in the world. It ain't right, it's just not right, but then that's how it goes, right. People don't care anymore. People don't care for other people. People don't have any compassion. All over the world in the church, out of the church they are all the same. Sometimes I just don't understand how we can have so much of you and yet allow ourselves to commit sins willfully. We say we walk with you daily, but then there can be no way when you just do something, because that is what was in your heart to do. Then even though they realize that they have been tricked, or whatever the case maybe, they don't stop and repent. They keep it up. "Ha, I guess I was the same way, because I was in the world for real, too." I'm tired Lord, and I need you to help me, I need you to start helping me get myself together. I can't do it by myself Lord. I can't do it without your help. You helped me before and I need you to help me again. I can't do it; I don't have the strength for it. I don't want to fight; I don't want to stand at the door with the knife. I don't want to be stalking at his job looking for him. I don't want to do any of it. I'm talking a good game right now, but I surely hope you help me. "Oh God! Please help me. Please help me." If you don't do nothing but give me the peace, just the peace through all this. So that this stuff don't worry or stress me, I will be so grateful. Wow this stuff will make a person lose their mine, and I don't want to do that. You have brought me too far. You brought me all the way here from the other Kathy. I did not get to this point in my life to die or go crazy. Not now because there are so many things that I want to do, things that I need to do. I can't do them if I'm not living, and I can't do them if I don't have peace of mind. I need to have peace of mind, you said that you would give us peace that surpasses all understanding, and God knows that is something that I need. Because right now there ain't nothing but hell going on up in here and hell needs to leave. Hell need to leave so the peace of God can come. I really need him to come and I'm not asking for him but I'm asking for myself. He has got to find his own. He has got to get his own, because I can't help him. I can't help myself so I know I can't help him. Don't really want to help him. But I'm going to talk to him and tell him that we need to tell the children about the divorce. That he and I can start living like we are really living, because we are merely existing. I'm tired of the lie. We are not a happily marry couple. I don't want to live like this no more. The entire family needs to know. Instead of you walking around here pretending that we are doing great, when you really are unhappy with me. Has been unhappy with me for some time. Well you would think that after all that talking to you Lord that I would feel more at ease, but I don't. Lord, thank you for allowing me to bend your ear. It was time for me to call Linda. I knew that she would be up and moving around. I picked up the phone and waited for Linda to answer.

"Linda, hi, What are you doing?

"Getting your brother-in-law's lunch and breakfast ready, so he can go to work," she said. What's up sissy? What's wrong?

"I'm having a bad morning and I don't know what to do about it. I'm going crazy Linda. Please talk to me please?"

"Sissy get in your car and come down here to us."

"I can't. My car might not make it that far, and I don't want to take that chance."

"Well hang-up, and call Stephanie and see if she will come and get you. See if she wants to meet me halfway or will she bring you to the house."

"Okay I'll call her, but I really don't want to put anyone out. Maybe I'll be okay until Stephanie comes by. She was supposed to come over for a while anyway."

"No sissy, you call her now and call me back."

"Okay, bye." I hung up and started to wonder if I had done the right thing.

I couldn't seem to get all of my thoughts in a single file line so I could think with some type of sense. Feeling apprehensive about what I was about to do, I did it anyway. I was afraid that if I left, Raymond would be angry with me. He would then bring those women into our home and sleep with them in our bed. I believed that was something that he had already done, so he would do it again, yet I picked up my cell and called Stephanie. For that split moment I realized that if I did not get away for just a day, I would be totally destroyed.

"Hello!"

"Ha Stephanie, I was wondering if you could come and get me please?"

"What's wrong Kathy, are you alright?"

"No Stephanie, I can't handle this today and I don't know what to do. I just need to get away from here."

"Okay let me get ready and I will be there as soon as I can."

"Thanks, I really do appreciate it. You just don't know how much. Let me call Linda back and tell her that you are coming."

I got off the phone with Stephanie. I really didn't want to call Linda back. I didn't want to talk anymore, but I did the right thing and called her back. I let her know that Stephanie would be coming to get me and she would bring me down there to Lakeland. Then she told me to bring all of my important papers with me, anything else I could think of. I just wanted to get away for awhile to calm down so that I could do some rational thinking. I told Linda I needed to get off the phone so I could concentrate.

I was so confused. I just began to throw anything into the suitcase. I started to feel as if my body was about to jump out of itself. Oh how I wished grandma was there with me. She would hold me in her arms and tell me that everything would be alright. For whatever reason I would believe what she said because grandma always knew how to make something bad in life turn out good. After I had packed everything that I thought I needed, I waited and in that waiting I became nervous, because Raymond was working different hours and I didn't know if he would come by the house before I could leave.

The fear of being caught trying to run started to get the best of me. I could not understand why I was afraid. I had every right to leave. Maybe it was the way I was leaving that bothered me. If I wanted to do something I just did it. I never tried to hide. This was different, very different. When I saw Stephanie pull up, all I wanted to do was run to the car with my stuff and get the hell out of there, but

Stephanie acted as if she was not in any rush. She acted as if we had all the time in the world.

She wanted to walk through the house and look around. She hadn't seen the house since we moved in. I forgot that she could not feel what I was feeling, so the need to leave was my own. I showed her around the house, not feeling anything but anxiety. We finally left the house. Even when we got into the car I was afraid that he would see us on the road. Stephanie had to keep reminding me that he would not be looking for her car. I remember when I couldn't wait to see Raymond on the road. It would make me light up like a Christmas tree, and sometimes I would turn around just to stop him and kiss his lips. I kept telling her that he would see me in her car and want to know where we were going. Plus, she did not have any tint on her windows. But she kept insisting that he would not, so I just kept my mouth closed and looked out the window.

"Kathy are you going to call David and Maxwell and let them know what's going on?"

"Yes, I will tell Maxwell everything and I will tell David only that we are having some problems. I dare not tell David that his father has stepped outside of our marriage. He is our hot head, and to tell him would cause more trouble and that is something that I just don't need. Once we get farther out I'll call the boys and talk to them and let them know that we love them and no matter what happens we will always love and be there for them.

I needed them to be the men that we raised them to be. David was okay but Maxwell was not and I think that was because I told him what was really going on. He was very upset saying that the reason I would have to go without was because his dad was taking from me and taking care of that bitch. He had to tell me that he was sorry, because he did not talk like that in front of me or on the phone. He told me that he had to go, but he would check on me later.

We got into Lakeland and drove up to Linda's house, but she hadn't made it there yet, so we waited. The wait was not long. She came flying up like she was going to a steak-out. We all said hello and hugged one another, and then they helped me get my things into the house.

Once I was settled in we all sat around the kitchen table and started talking about what was going on. Then Linda told me how Raymond would call her daughter and talk about me like a dog. That would hurt because all that stuff he would say to me would be a lie. I didn't realize that Raymond disliked me so, I thought that I had done all I knew to do. To make him happy. He was telling her that I was all about the money. That I wouldn't work and that he had given the best years of his life to the boys and me. Now it was time for him. That he didn't get the things he wanted because of me. That tore my heart even more because I always talked to Raymond and if he felt that strongly about things, Why didn't he say so? He was making me the heavy again, like he always did. My mind began to reflect on things that transpired in our marriage. It was the same when I left to go up and take care of my mom. All the bills were paid, except the rent and car payment. The first week I was gone, I kept after Raymond to pay the rent. The house had been stocked with food. I had cooked up some food and put it in the freezer. All clothes were ironed, and the house was clean. They would need only milk, eggs, bread, other cold-cuts, but as far as anything else they would be okay.

I didn't know until I had been back for a month and I got a note on the door of the condo, that the rent check for the month that I left bounced. Needless to say that put us into a tight for the next three months, and Raymond said it was because he had to take care of me while I was in Atlanta. That was not it. It was that he was taking care of that woman and taking from our home to do it. It made a lot of things clear now. It was her or someone else all the time. Instead of being truthful and doing what was right, he put the blame on me. Sometimes it does not matter how long you have been with a person, you never know them.

Linda had to go to the drug store to pick up her medicine. She wanted to know if we wanted to stay at her place until she got back. I told her yes; then I told her no. Stephanie and I got up and went with Linda. While she was doing that Stephanie was looking at cards, and I was looking for a particular soap, when my phone rang.

"Hey baby boy, 'what's up?"

"Mama I just wanted to call you back and tell you, whatever you decide to do I will support you because I love you and you will always be our superwoman and you don't have to settle."

The tears began to fall and I could not stop them, and then all the pain that was within me rose to the surface. All the strength left in my body was gone. I couldn't even continue to stand. Stephanie and Linda were at my side and they helped me out of the store. The tears and pain just continued to come. They finally got me into the car. I didn't want anyone to see me cry like that. Only God knew how deep the pain went. I wanted no one to witness my shame. But they did and I could hear Stephanie crying in the back and Linda could only hold my hand. I willed the pain to leave, but it wouldn't. It had made a place in my heart, and it would not let go. I thought that I would die at that very moment. No one spoke a word; we just kept our thoughts to ourselves. What could one do when someone you love is in pain at this magnitude?

When we returned to the house, I just sat back at the table. I couldn't bring myself to look at anyone, so I kept my head down. Stephanie sat across from me and Linda started to get a little dinner ready. Linda asked if I wanted something to eat.

I told her that I had no appetite.

"Well, you still need to try and eat something," said Stephanie.

She wanted to know when I had eaten last, and when I told her it was two days ago, she insisted that I would eat she fixed me something and assured me that when I ate something she would leave me alone, so I ate some of the food. Anything to get Stephanie off my back. I found that I was more hungry than I thought, and the food was very tasty. We just sat and talked more and waited for Linda's husband to come home from work. Cody is Raymond's oldest brother. Cody and I had it out but when the dust settled. We became fast friends. Cody is a straight and truthful man. He is a minister and really tries to live up to what it means to be a man of God. You can't help but have respect for him. He is not perfect but he is fair. We wanted Cody to pray for me and Stephanie before she went home. When he came in Cody did just that.

The prayer was just what I needed. I could feel the pressure of all the pain and worrying go away. I felt for the first time since this whole thing started that I would be able to get some sleep. Stephanie left and Linda, Cody and I went back into the house. Cody got into his favorite chair and went to sleep, while Linda and I went into the kitchen.

I helped her clean the kitchen. Then Linda got ready for bed because she had to go to work in the morning. I took my bath and said good night to everyone. I laid down in the bed and thought that I would be able to fall asleep quickly, but sleep did not come easily. I laid on my back and thought about what Raymond was doing. Was he at home missing me or was he with her tonight? I knew that I could not allow myself to think like that, so I turned on the television. I tried to find something to watch that would keep my mind from going places. It did for awhile, but I soon realized that I didn't want to watch anything that was on.

Sleep finally came and even though it was not eight hours of sleep, it was the best sleep I had, in a long time. I was up at four, and the first thing I thought of was Raymond. I was ready to go home, and it didn't matter what things were like at home. I was ready to go. I wanted to look at him, and I wanted him to hold me. This was some crazy shit. I felt one way one minute and another the next. I thought that I was ready to give Raymond the divorce and move on with my life, so I made sure that I called my mom and sisters to let them know what I was about to do. I thought I was really ready to do this, so when my sister-in-law got off work, we left.

I called Raymond to let him know that I was coming home. He wanted to know the time. I told him I'd be there by nine o'clock. That was the longest ride of my life. When we pulled into the driveway he was bringing the trash can from the road. When he reached the car he spoke to me, then to his brother and sister-in-law. He then helped me with my stuff. I wanted to jump into his arms and just love on him. I felt like a fool, thinking that I was ready to do this, and the minute I saw his face, all I wanted to do was to love him, and make my life happy the way I thought it had been.

When they left, we went into the house and I began to tell him what I had decided to do. He did not want that. He felt that maybe we just needed some time apart and I felt the only reason he wanted that was that he would be free to see that woman. If that was the case then I felt that there was no point in dragging this on. The sooner we got this over with the sooner I could go through and move on with what life I would have left.

For the next week or two, we talked and made love as if for the first time. We had blow ups and we had tears, but through all of that, nothing was changing. He still wanted to see other women and go to the clubs without me. He still wanted to have sex with other women, yet he wanted me to put my life on hold until he knew what he really wanted to do.

One night about 3:00 in the morning my spiritual mother called, we both sat straight up in the bed. First we thought that it was a call about my dad. I got up and went to the dresser to look at my phone. It was Pastor Bullard. Why in the world was she calling at this time of morning? I answered the phone and she asked to speak to Raymond.

When she finished talking with him, she asked to speak to me. She told me to read Psalm 15 every day and to get some oil to anoint every window and door. She also told me to pray for my husband and to hang in there. I said I would, but in my heart I was saying the hell with that. I would do all of what she asked except the praying for him. Hell, I needed prayer for myself! Whatever she said to him gave him a wakeup call, or so it seemed. When we did get up, we prayed and read the bible just as she had asked.

Then Raymond went to work and I went to the store to get the oil so Pastor Bullard could pray over it. When I called her back, she told me that she had a dream where the Lord showed her Raymond dying with AIDS. He would be coming to me to take care of him. I told her that he should let whoever he got it from take care of him, and I told her that when I walk away it will be for good. I don't ever want to see, hear, or talk to him again. I wish him all the best in life, but I would like to just forget this part of my life, as much as possible. Pastor Bullard then told me that someone had put witchcraft on him and she needed me to give her a week to break some of those spirits off of him. I told her I would try, because I knew that I would take all the help that I could get. But things did not get better, because he continued to visit with that other woman and talk to her over the phone.

Whenever he came home, he always acted as if life with me was peaches and cream. Now how mucked up is he? He thinks he has all the sense in the world and he's dumb as shit. We had more talks. Not that they did us any good. He even had the nerve to tell me that he thought he was a good judge of character. He didn't really believe what Pastor Bullard said. I just looked at him trying to figure out how the hell he thinks he is a good judge of character. This hoe can't even keep his pig in his pants, and not only that. Raymond is supposed to be a man of God and a minister at that. How the hell could he possibly think that he can be a good judge of character? See that just goes to show you just how mucked up he is. Well we moved as well as anyone could I guess.

What I needed now was my grandmother's God. So I decided to have a heartfelt and earnest conversation with the Lord.

Lord, you know what I realized two months after I found out what my husband did! I realized while making up our bed that I don't know how to desire you Lord, the way I desire Raymond. That's a wow factor! I don't know how to just give my whole heart to you. I now realize that I want to, I really want to! I need you to teach me how to want you, because I don't know how to do it without you, Lord. I don't know how to pull myself to you, and I need you. I need you to do that for me. I need you to draw me in a way that I have never ever been drawn before. I need you to do that, I don't want to desire Raymond the way I used to. I don't ever want to desire another human being like that. I want and I need to desire you like that. (I was so overwhelmed that I was moved to tears.)

When you realize Lord that the person you should have been loving like that, the one who has always been there, the one who has seen to your every need. You realize that you don't desire them like that. It has to be more devastating to you than anything in this world. All I can say is Lord, I am so sorry. I am so, so sorry! I don't know how to love you like that, but I am willing. If it means that I don't ever have to be hurt by people again (I made a sound of almost laughter) Yes, yes you and I can go for it! We can truly go for it. You know it's like being stripped of everything I know, everything that I believe in. I am standing here trying to figure out who am I, what am I, why am I here, what is my purpose.

All those years I been living this life and I thought I knew the answer to all of those questions and then I got slapped so hard, that I don't even know who I am anymore. I looked around and I thought that my life, my presence everything about me was different from the other people, the other couples I see, the ones that I come in contact with. All the time I was thinking that what I had was real, because I dealt with our issues, by putting them on the table. We quarreled; I stood my ground, gave in at times and I thought that if I was open, then Raymond would be open, but what I found was that was not the case. We were just like every other family. Couples sometimes pretend that their life is something that it is not, and I don't want that, Lord. I want my marriage as well as my spiritual marriage to be real. Oh God! Be so real you know! Not that we have to act like a fool, but I want it to be so real until people can feel the very presence of it. It's amazing, Oh God it's just amazing. I don't know where I got that from or why but AH! I want people to see you in us. NO matter what road we are going down, but that in us it will be real. It will be real in us. We don't need to be validated or approved or anything by people, because what we'll have between us will be so deep and so oh my God I can't even describe it. But people will not understand that, unless they have had it. Lord, let us experience, and be in the presence of love like that! They can't help wanting you, too Lord. They can't help but oh Jesus! Oh God you have got to help me. You have to help me. We're not perfect. No we're not perfect, but to be so real to be so open to be so true. God that's wow! I don't even know when I have ever felt something like that before. I cannot recall ever in my life experiencing something as deep as that. (Again I am so overwhelmed with emotion that I can't stop the tears from falling. With each revelation the emotion becomes more and more intense.) I know that I have felt that before because of you, and that is how I know it. I want it, I want it, Wow this is amazing. Oh Jesus, Oh God!

I thought that I was okay. It was now the beginning of March and I was still here, still confused and still emotional. I wasn't living, I was just existing and doing the things that were common to me. People can do things a way for so long until it's just like breathing every day, they just do it without thinking. So to me even though I knew that my emotions were upside down I still thought I was doing good, but I wasn't. Raymond was right; I didn't realize that I had stopped doing things. My mind did not seem to be there. I was regressing. I lost a part of me and I was not trying to find it. I would have to open myself up to be hurt in that capacity again and that was not going to happen. All the things that I do, I don't even think about them sometimes and that is not good. I need to be able to. I have just shut down, I can't even describe it. I am lost. Something was stolen from me and I don't know how to get it back. I don't know how to find it. Even if I did, I don't know if I would allow myself to open up to Raymond again because I'm sacred as hell.

I don't want to start living and it's not right, or real. I don't want to live a life that I don't really have. I understand that now. These things don't mean anything to me. They meant something only because we use to be us. Yes he's working hard, but it used to be us. I don't feel like that anymore and I'm, trying to find my way back home.

I remember once when Raymond's mother told him that he was crazy to allow me to have access or control his money. For a long time he didn't pay her any attention, or so I thought, but the day came when he did away with the one account and we no longer shared. He had his and I my own. I did help bring about that change, because like so many wives, we spend when we should not, but while I was spending and most of it always went to the home. Raymond was spending too on his investment deals that never pan out or on his mom and siblings. We both were doing wrong even if we thought we had a right. It's really, really hard to do, Lord. Raymond was the closest person to Christ for me. He never judged me. He had his opinion about me, but he didn't judge. He looked beyond something and he saw what I had tried to keep hidden. From there love began to grow. When he told me to hold on to God, no matter, I took what he said and started to work with it. I realized that I had begun to let things go. I didn't have the will to fight, at least not in the way that I should. I wish I trusted one human being to the point that I could go to them and really get the help I need. I'm finding in the walk of life there is not one, that I can tell my deepest and darkness secrets. No one to help me and it stay just between us and God.

Raymond and I got up on Monday morning. We had breakfast, and he got his conference call. When all was done we dressed and left the house, checked on something and took care of something. When we finished we headed back home, when both our phones rang. I finished my call first, so I was able to listen to his conversation. I knew that he was talking to that woman or her daughter. More into the conversation I knew that it was the girl. She was not feeling well, and she wanted him to take her to the hospital. He asked her if she was pregnant and she told him she didn't know. He asked her if she'd had sex, and she told him that she had about three weeks ago. He told her that he was with his wife, and she said that was sweet. He told her that he could not do it right then, but when he was done with me, he would come. Raymond then explained the phone conversation to me. I told him he could drop me off at the house and go on. I was already on pins and needles just waiting for something to happen.

This was something to ruined our day as something did most times. Whatever joy I was feeling had now been killed. I wanted to do lunch with him, but I knew that when it was over, he would leave me for her. He got off the phone with her and told me that he wanted to take me to that new restaurant he told me about. I told him that he didn't have to do that and he could take me home and go ahead. We went to lunch, and could not eat my food, so he dropped me off at the house. The last thing he told me was that he loved me. I could not see the love at the time, because love would not have done what he had just done. It was about 4p.m. when he left. I did not even watch him drive away. He only gets two days off, and he usually spends them catching up on his sleep or in his office. Except for those two, he is usually gone. The hell with me. How could he say he loved me, yet with the same breath, leave me for the women he would sleep with? He was always too tired, or at least when it came to me. When he had already had sex with the other woman before he came home to me.

He was always too tried for sex, and if he wasn't, I had to initiate and do all the work. Then I would think wow! I tried to find things to take my mind off the fact that my husband was with a girl that I thought he may have fathered. He could even be the father of her child, if in fact we find out that they slept together too. I couldn't sit home any longer. I got in my car and left. Riding and looking, not for my husband, but for someone else. I knew that my husband would not be in this area, so I wasn't worried about running into him. I wanted someone to talk to, to listen to me, to distract me from all the things that were going on in my life. When I couldn't find who I was looking for, I just decided to go to the park and sit. My son called and we talked about me, him, our marriages, and some of the things that we wanted to do. Then I drove back home and watched a movie on the DVD.

You can't make someone want you. You can't change them. I can't pretend that this is not happening. So I have to do something so I can cope with this. I changed into my shorts and went for my walk. It began to rain and I was so far from home that I had to wait for it to stop raining, before I could go home. I had to put my phone and my keys in my panties. It's a good thing that I didn't put on a little less. I had to run back to the store I had just left. I waited for the rain to stop, so I could make it back to the house. I was soaked from head to toe. It had also gotten darker than I had wanted it to be. I didn't want to run into any animals. I finally got home and jumped into the shower. After the shower I got a glass of wine, sat in front of the television and tried to watch another movie.

It was now around 9p.m. and Raymond text and asked me to print off directions to Miami. I told him that it was already done. I had collected everything that I thought he would need on tomorrow. He thanked me and I said nothing. I went to bed, praying that sleep would overtake me and I would not have to think about what Raymond was doing or know what time he got home. As much as I tried sleep would not come. At about 9:33p.m. he sent another text:

Baby I am so sorry!!!!!!!!!! I should not have gotten into this. I should have known how you really felt. Seriously, I should not have gotten into this.

I texted back, *"If you really were sorry you would not still be there."*

I don't know when the next text came. I just know that he said they were getting ready to let her go, and he would be home. I did not respond. I tried to get some sleep again, but again it would not come. I got up and looked at the clock and realized that it was midnight. I knew that I couldn't do it anymore. I put on some clothes and left the house. I thought about going to the hospital and going inside just to make a scene. I decided that no good would come of that. I would possibly be the one to get in trouble behind this, so I just didn't bother. I passed the hospital without looking back. I first drove to the park and looked out at the water. I felt compelled to call my friend but I thought better of it. I decided to go riding instead.

Around 12:30a.m. my phone rang and it was Raymond. I thought it would be better not to answer, but I did.

"Hello."

"Hi baby, where are you?"

"I'm riding."

"Come home baby, please."

"Okay Raymond."

I went home but not right away. I wasn't ready to look at him or hear more lies come out of his mouth. I didn't want to be treated like a fool again. I couldn't take anything else from Raymond. That was it for me, as that old saying goes this was the straw that broke the camel's back. Now I wanted the Lord to do whatever he wanted to do. I didn't care anymore. I just want my peace back. I wanted him to knock it out the ball park. I wanted this over, but only God's way, so I would not have to do this again. I wanted out, I wanted out of this lie of a marriage, relationship, everything that it meant. I wanted out of it. Something other than this had to be better. It's about the peace. It has always been about the peace.

Raymond made his promises of what he was going to do, "ya, okay, if you say so baby." He said he was going to make things right. He said that he was going to fix it. Okay if that's what you say then you fix it, cause I'm through. He was just going to tell more lies and make more promises. I just don't want to hear it anymore. I just don't want to be bothered.

I'm so through with it. I can't do it anymore. I don't want to do it anymore. All I want is for God to do what he's going to do and let me go. That's all; that's all. I can't make him do or be anything. What Raymond does has to come from his heart. If it's not there, then it can't nor will it come. Raymond will have to need and want this with me.

Everything he showed me was contrary to what came out of his mouth. I can't do anything with that, and I won't. I deserve to be loved the way I think that I should be. I deserve the same kind of love that I have given him. It is amazing; oh my God! it is amazing. I am really through this time. He could do whatever he wanted to. It was his business. I can't do anything about it anyway. I can't stop him. I'm not going to fight with him. It will be just what it will be. It still didn't change the fact that I loved him. I still love him, when we really truly allow ourselves to step out of the way, we find that there is more God in us than we realize.

When we went to bed he held me very closely, as if I might run at anytime. I was not going anywhere, at least not that night. I was mentally tired and all I wanted was to get some sleep. I fell asleep in his arms and when I woke up I was still in his arms. As soon as I opened my eyes all the pain came back. I picked it up right where I left it the night before. So much for a beautiful Wednesday morning! I knew that Raymond would have to answer some questions for me. I felt that secrets were still being kept, so after he went to work I sent him a text.

I asked him if there were any more surprises coming that I should know about. Now I had just said the day before that I was through. Right! Well, so much for that strength, because I was not feeling it today. I was trying to hang on to something that I thought I had. This is where that line of is this insanity or is it love becomes blurred. It just makes me think that I am crazy as hell. I hoped that everything was out in the open. I was not trying to upset him. I also didn't understand why I would be worried about upsetting him, when he gave me no thought at all. Anyway, I went on to say that it just felt that I was being punished for something that I didn't do and I don't know why. I never expected him to text or call me. I figured that he would do as he has always done; he would not answer. When he showed up at the house, I would wonder what was up with that.

When he came in, he spoke and went into the office. About 20 minutes later he came out and asked me to join him. I stopped ironing and stood in front of him. He addressed my text. He told me that I did nothing wrong. He was finding out just how messed up and bad he was. He told me that he had been sleeping with three other women since we have been married. I could feel the tears in the back of my eyes, but they did not run down my face. I stood there thinking that the last 20 years of our life had been a lie, but it really was, and it put things on a different playing field. I stood there and listened to him tell me this stuff. I can't even begin to tell you what goes through a woman's mind. So much was coming; I couldn't even keep up with it. Raymond looked me in the eyes and told me again to let him fix it. Let him straighten this mess that he created. When he left, I couldn't go back to ironing. My head was full of all the things that he had just told me. When we got together, he led me to believe that he had never had sex before, and that I was his first and that he was all mine.

The truth was that he already belonged to another and another. I was the only fool walking around thinking that he was the man for me. A man that I could grow to know, without the sex. We would become really good friends. I thought that our relationship started on truth, when it was so far from that. It all started out as a lie and that is what made our marriage a lie. He married me knowing that he would sleep with other women and he knew that was the one thing that I told him that I couldn't do. He acted as if we were the perfect couple. We were living a life that was not true. It made me think about the things that his mother said to me. I had caused her son to walk away from God and made him do things that he would not normally do. Little did she know that her precious son was already doing those things and he was doing them long before I came along, but then I wonder just how much she already knew. I don't even know what happen to the rest of that day, let alone the rest of the week. It all was just a blank. I just went through it, not feeling a thing. I tried not to think about what Raymond had told me. For me to do that would be to deal with all the emotion, and I just was not ready for that. If I could have buried my head in the sand I would have done so.

If a woman is true to herself, she cannot just let it go at that. It was time to find out who these hoes were since he wanted to keep them a secret. I knew one had to be Jonita. She was the supervisor that worked with him. I could not say for sure, but I knew there was something between the two. I'm not sure about Candice either. Had she slept with Raymond or is she holding out like Jonita? When Jonita needs Raymond he just runs to her rescue. That witch needs to stay away from my husband. Then there was Cassandra Devane Davis, the friend that he had since high school she is the bitch that he allowed into our home, while I was with my dad. She is the one I think he slept with in our home, but he says he did not. If a man goes to the trouble of cooking dinner for a woman in his home and he thinks that you would believe that was all he did, who is the fool? The daughter of Cassandra, little Miss Khymesha Davis, is the one that he took to the hospital. I felt that he was fucking her to. He said that she went both ways. He did ask her if she might be pregnant. At this point I did not think that it would be anything that Raymond wouldn't do.

Oh but please let us not forget the number one bitch, the root working Wanda Reed King, whom he has been having the longest relationship with. This is the one that he spent vacation time with, the one that fed him stuff that would help him to leave. These things that I found out, I kept to myself until I was ready to let Raymond know that I knew by name and where they lived.

Raymond told me one day that I could not handle the truth, but I think I am dealing with more truth than he realizes. I may have my moments of crazy, but don't let that fool you. I still think like a woman. I know now just how much he was lying and cheating. When he said that he had to work long hours, he was with the other women. When he was supposed to be working or taking a lunch break, he was with the other women. When he had to go into work early, he was with the other women. When he said that he was going one place, he went another with women. When he took that girl to the hospital because she was sick, he thought that she was pregnant with his baby. He will never admit to it, and he doesn't have to. He believes that allowing me to think whatever I want is the best thing. Then he could be saying that I won't believe him anyway. That may be true, but he should do more talking to me and less letting me think on my own.

Sunday was our wedding anniversary. Nineteen years, and we couldn't even tell each other happy anniversary (I laughed only to keep from crying).

Raymond said, "I want to tell you Happy Anniversary, but because of what is going on, where we are is not happy."

He was so right. He held me in his arms, and I held him back. Then I asked him, "Why, why did you choose me, Raymond? You could have had any of them, so why me?"

"You were the one, who took the time. You were the one who cared and hung in there with me. I fell in love with you."

I thought to myself, "Shit if this is your love then damn I would hate to see you hate." I could do nothing only repeat that statement in my head. I was the one who hung in there and took the time. There never should have been a relationship between us, just the sex. I was not looking for a man to love or have in my life, just someone I wanted for the moment. Can you think of any man seeing my body and my willingness to give myself just like that would have jumped at the chance, but not this one. He didn't know me well enough to just have sex and go. It was not a problem, because it wasn't like I was in love with the man. It was almost two years before we had sex. Anyway, by the time he realized that the other women wanted him it was too late. He had gotten with me and he fell in love. He didn't want to let me go, and so here we are. Still sticking and hanging, but we don't know if we will make it through this.

I said, "You knew that you were not ready for this kind of life. Why couldn't you have just walked away. You knew that you were not going to do right by me, so why not just leave me alone."

"I couldn't Kathy I knew that if I asked you to wait and I walked away to do the things that I wanted to do, you would not be here waiting for me. I was not willing to take that chance of losing you."

"So you were being selfish and you never gave any thought to the fact that you would deeply hurt me?"

"I thought I would be able to control my demons."

"Ok, but when you saw that your demons were winning, did it even occur to you that maybe you should get some help?"

"No, because I knew what my problem was. I just didn't know how to fix it."

"Wow! So you know how to fix it now?"

"No, but I will do what I have to so that this will not destroy what we have."

We began to touch each other in ways that people who don't know one another's body touch each other. The love making was bitter sweet. It was love making of what we had, of what we had lost and what we were trying to find again. To no avail, it was not found that day. Raymond took me to dinner for our anniversary. After dinner we saw a movie and tried to make this day as special as it should have been. It didn't work because no matter how much he tried, he had allowed other women to come into our world and I didn't know how to push them out so that he and I could enjoy one another again. Even though they were not with us, their presence was always around. It became unbearable for me, because I could never get away from them. I thought of what they must have talked about while he was driving them somewhere or was she holding his hand while he was driving? Was it the same way I hold his hand or touch it? When I touch him, is he thinking of her and not me. Thoughts and pain of wondering and never really knowing were endless. He was not telling because he doesn't know what it is like to feel or think this way. Needless to say it was just a day. It was what it was, no more, no less. We came home after the movie. Raymond went to his office and I went into the bedroom to be tormented by the demons that haunted me when I was alone. I wasn't tormented for long because my phone made a sound. It was a text from Stephanie.

"Hi, how are you doing today?"

"I've seen better days."

"Is Raymond home?"

"Yes."

"Can I call you in a little while?"

"Yes, but I won't be able to talk.

"Hope your day was ok."

"My day was bad; Raymond was talking to his girl Saturday."

"Not good."

"Ya!"

"I wish I knew what to tell you, but one thing I do know is that you have to decide what is best and sometimes that decision is not the easiest."

"Just trying to enjoy what I can."

"Maybe you enjoy being with him, but the question is what does he enjoy?"

"I think that he enjoys what he is doing. He wants to continue to see and talk to this woman."

"So what direction is he leaning towards?"

"He said that he didn't see her long term in his future, but he saw us that way."

"Don't understand?"

"He isn't ready to decide what he wants to do. But he wants his marriage to work. He even told me if I couldn't get pass this, then we would not make it. He didn't know how long he would be willing to go through this. He also said that she told him that he needed to decide who he wanted to be with, because she wants to be with him."

"Evidently, he cares about you both, but maybe for different reasons."

"I know and that is what hurts. He can't see that he cares for her more than he cares for us."

"Maybe he does see it and that is why it is difficult for him to make up his mind."

"Since he won't decide, then I have to, even if I am not ready."

"Sounds like both of you are beneficial to him. He does not have any obligations with her and he is able to let his hair down figuratively speaking."

"I am going to have to see a lawyer even though that is not what I want to do. He does not leave me any choice, because he won't make up his mind."

"Just make sure you seek God and be sure that the decision is one of peace."

"I think this will be one of the hardest to make, and I know if it is the wrong decision, I will let myself down. I can't live like this Stephanie, and I won't."

"Let me know what you decide."

"Okay, will have to finish later. He is ready to go. Thanks for being you."

Everything is going to be alright! Just let God be what only he can be in your life and through your life. Stop warring with yourself. Use your energy wisely so the process can be effortless.

"I will try, but you may have to remind me."

"I surely will if you need me to."

"Thanks as always."

It always helped talking to Stephanie. She somehow helped me to make sense of what was going on in my life and it helped me to bear things just a little more. I can't say that things got better or things got worse. I knew that I needed to leave. I just couldn't bring myself to do it. So I did started asking the Lord to tell me what to do. I needed God to help me. What I needed from him all the time was his help.

One night in my sleep he told me to wait on him. He told me to trust him. I need to, but I really don't want to, because to wait on him and to trust him is to surrender everything that I feel, everything that goes through my mind. I have to give in to it completely. It's like I see this runaway train and I know that it's going to crash, but still I have to stay on that train, and I ride until it comes to a complete stop, or he fix whatever is wrong, and that is a hard thing to do, but I have to do it. What else am I supposed to do? Am I to say no, Lord, I'm not going to trust you. I'm not going to believe what you say. Even though there is a little part of me that wants to say it, I know who I am, but do I really know what I am talking about. It's hard, but that's the way it is, especially when I walk with the Lord, especially when he says wait on him. Instead of me taking charge and doing what I need to do, because I am the one feeling this pain. I am the one suffering. I am the one that can't sleep and can't eat. I am the one that's crying. Nobody really understands. Nobody really knows how it feels. I hear people, but I don't hear them, because would they really say this if they were in my shoes. What a wow question. I should have asked myself that same question before it happen to me.

I thought I just needed to clear my head and since Raymond's vacation was coming up that would be a good time to get away. He had stopped telling me about his vacation time until the last minute because he was spending that time with the other women. I knew that we had to go to Miami first to see about a business deal. I knew that if everything worked out, we would be going to Atlanta. This was fine with me because I just needed to get way from here, and we went. We left on a Thursday morning and as we made our way farther out of state it felt good. I could feel the tension and the pressure roll away from my shoulders, mind and body. It was just wonderful. Anyway Raymond was thinking so hard because you could see the lines and the light the way it hit and missed his eyes. His lips were turned into the corner of his face. I wanted to know what he was thinking, so I asked him.

"I'm thinking about you?"

"What about me, you were thinking?"

"I was thinking how I hurt you. I didn't realize just how hard it was going to be for you to get through this."

I'm listening to him, but I really don't know what to think or believe. I know what my heart wants to believe. I know what my mind tells me what to believe. My heart is not in sync with my head. So I say okay.

"I was also thinking about your friend."

"So okay what about my friend?"

"I don't know maybe you want to go and be with him."

"No I can't say that it hasn't crossed my mind, but I know what I want, and I know who I want to be with. I just don't know if they want to be with me. We talked about me talking to another guy. We knew what that could lead to, even if I don't mean for it to. I understood everything he said.

He told me that whatever I decided to do, he wasn't going anywhere. He would be right here when I got back. I told him that he was crazy as hell. If he expected me to tell him something like that, he would be waiting a long time, because I could never tell him something like that. That is not what will happen. I will not be here when he came back. I wouldn't want to be here when he came back. I couldn't do anything but laugh a little bit. He seemed to mean what he was saying. Sometimes I don't know what touches him. I don't know what doesn't touch him. I thought I knew a little about him in twenty years, but I found out I don't.

We rode on and we talked a little more, and the farther away we got the more relaxed he and I became. I began to have just a little more peace. I hadn't felt like that for some months oh ya! oh ya! I was ready. My God, I was ready to be away from there. He drove all the way. I didn't have to help at all. It was good. When we got to town, we made a few stops, picked up some things, and then we went on to the house. We saw Dad and Mom and my mom's girlfriend Roxie from North Carolina. We put things in and away and headed out again. When we finished, we headed back to the house. It was fun. We had laughs. I felt good to be at ease with him. I felt good not to have to look over my shoulder and wonder if the next woman I looked at could be one that he fucked. It felt like he belonged only to me again and that felt really good.

The following morning we got up, packed an overnight bag and headed out again. Raymond took me to Pine Mountain, Georgia. He made reservations for an overnight stay. We got there around 12p.m. and checked-in. We had a lodge room. It was like a hotel room, but it looked as if we had stepped into a log cabin. It was a beautiful place with a king size bed, with a handmade quilt. A rocking chair sat by the big window, so we could look out and see the valley, the trees and animals below. The room was separate with its own private bath. The bath was a red heart shaped Jacuzzi tub for two. It was like nothing that I had seen before. We got settled in and it was he and I for the rest of the day.

No one saw or heard from us until we returned. It was as if we had traveled in time and all our problems and troubles did not exist. We had fun and laughs. We enjoyed each other, just one moment at a time. We did not expect anything. It felt so good, so exuberating. It was a wonderful weekend. I let Raymond know that I enjoyed being with him. I enjoyed our time together just us. Nobody else, nothing else, just us and it was good, really good!

When I realized that we had to go back home, my peace went, when I truly realized that we had to come back here. For just a little while my life was good. I was in love again. It was like living a fairytale, which came to a screeching halt. Oh God the peace was really gone then! The tension, the worry, the frustration all came back, and I could hardly sleep. I tossed and turned all night long, knowing that I had to come back to this hell of a life, which I had. Oh Jesus, it was just too much! For any person, at least for me. I cried. Oh God I cried!

I walked that Saturday morning that we were going to leave. I told my mom, I don't want to go back. The tears started to come. I don't want to go back with him Mama; I just don't want to go back. That thing hit me like a ton of bricks. I didn't want to go back home with him because I didn't want to leave the peace. I didn't want to leave the serenity, just living, just living a peaceful life.

"Kathy, babe, please stop crying. Everything will work out. You'll see.

"Mama, I don't want to see."

"Kathy you are making me cry."

"I'm sorry, but I feel like I'm dying all over again."

"You can make it, and the Lord will help you."

"I don't want the Lord to help me. I just want him to let me stay here."

"Then you will give those women a chance to come in and really take over."

"No, Raymond did that already remember!"

Mama just held my hand for a while and continued to walk without saying a word. I just kept thinking that it was wonderful and I did not want to leave it. I was willing to give him and everything up just to keep the peace that I had a couple of days ago. I really didn't want this, but we came back. All the emotion, drama, the headaches, body aches and the tears, anger, rage, everything just came back. Everything was waiting for my return. It was just waiting patiently.

When we returned, we just fell back into things again. Raymond was still seeing those women and he wanted me to be understanding about it all. He didn't get as angry about things as before, but he still told me that he didn't know how long he could do this. He did this but he was trying to make me rush and deal with this, yet he was still seeing those women and I was supposed to be okay with that. He didn't see anything wrong with keeping his fuck buddies as friends. As long as he was not sleeping with them it was okay and I should have been okay with it, also. He even went as far to tell me that he thought about having a baby with the daughter of one of the women he had been screwing. I asked him, how did you think I was going to feel. He told me that he didn't care that he was going to raise his child with or without me. Now if that shit didn't knock the wind out of my sail I don't know what would. It was at that moment that I began to wonder if Raymond had been wearing a condom while on his sexual escapades. So I asked Raymond about it.

"No Kathy, I didn't, not all the time."

"So it wasn't enough that you fucked outside our marriage, but you also put my life at risk."

"I was not trying to put your life at risk. I just never thought about it."

"Well, we both can tell that you didn't give it any thought. So now I have to go and be tested for HIV. All because you wanted to be a hoe, Raymond."

"I'm sorry Kathy," he said with a blank look on his face.

How do you continue to love a man, when he takes you through what he has taken me and continue to take me through? How do you keep the passion and desire all those things you once held so dear? I wish someone would tell me. I felt so humiliated. I had to go to that clinic on Thursday and sit there and tell those two women with my wedding ring on my finger, that I need to be tested for HIV, because I might have Aids. They seemed nice enough. They were even friendly, but it made the sting no less painful. They needed to ask me a series of questions. They needed to know how many sex partners I had. They wanted to know how I have sex? Did I go both ways? Those are things that I should not have to share with anyone. I might share some things with my girl, but even she has limits. I will never tell the juicy details, to strangers except when I am put in a position where I have to tell it. Now it's a matter of life and death. That is something that should not even be, not ever, especially not at this point in my life, in my marriage. The tears began to fall and I didn't bother to wipe them, because that was something that I should not have been going through. We should have been so far removed from this point in our life, but we weren't, so there we are where we are. How do you keep loving with the same love, the same passion, the same desire?

Raymond showed more concern for those women when I called them bitches than he did when I told him that I was going for the Aids test. Every time I make a left or right turn, I get kicked between the ass. I don't understand it, but such is life.

When I left there, I went straight home. I did not want to be seen by anyone. By the time I got home, my cell phone was ringing. It was Raymond wanting to know how I was doing. I don't think that he is really concern about the fact that I went. I think he did that because he probably felt it would be good right now to show some type of interest. I feel this because of the way he responds. He's so a loof when it comes to his feelings. I can't tell when he is really upset unless he wants me to know. So now I take nothing for granted. I don't assume anything, because it does not get me anywhere. I always ask now, because I don't know.

Oh Lord, this is hard, but I know you got me. You told me you got me and I believe you. I really, thank you. The nurse told me that it would be six weeks before the diagnosis from the test came back. Trying to be positive about the test was hard as hell. I wanted to think that I got by without being scared more than I already was. At the same time, I didn't want to be more of a fool than I already was.

I had not gotten the test results back yet, but other things came up whereas I didn't have to focus on me. My sister had to have surgery, and my mom came so she would be here to take care of my sister. I was glad that she would be here. I knew having her here would make things good for me. It does not matter how old you get when things go wrong in your life you always want your mama around to give you advice and to listen to you. Mama was always good about those things. She never was one of those parents who didn't know how to keep her nose out of people's business. She never just invited herself in without an invitation.

Mama had to pick me up the day after my sister's surgery because my car was in the shop. On our way to the hospital with my mom, as we drove away from the house.

I said to her, "You know Mama, when I look at this house it's like making it, yet never really getting there."

That means that we always seem to do a little better, but then there's that thing of where we don't do or could have done better, and it held us back. When we arrived my sister was ready for surgery. We were able to go back and sit with her until the doctor was ready. We talked about how dusty the room was and laughed about our upbringing. We wanted her to be calm and relaxed. This was her very first anything in the hospital. When they did come get her, we went and had breakfast, then returned to the waiting room. Everything went just find. Not once did we leave her alone. Someone stayed the night with her.

Raymond had come up to the hospital to be with us. I thanked him for that, because he really didn't have to do that. When I left it was with Raymond and I thought about the things mom and I talked about. I pray that one day we will be able to get that right. It's not about the material things. I mean if God is going to bless us and spiritually we are supposed to grow. Then I think that it's only fitting that it manifests itself. "Wow! That's what it is being able to take what has been done spiritually and let it work its way out." And that is how people see God's wondrous works through us. That's how they see it. I guess in order for us to do those things, we are going to have to do it. If you think about the ramifications of this and the process, you come to realize that this has to be done and done right.

Even though I say that I believed God had me, I couldn't tell. Because what did I go and do the very thing that would make one not believe anything I just said. Sometimes we say things and we mean them but we are so far from them. In my heart I even believed what I was saying. It's just my head didn't get it, or vice verses. Because I realized that I was on my way to falling really fast. Oh God I had not realized just how far I had already fallen. That's what you mean when you say don't harden your heart. You don't care how you come; I just better know that it's you when you do. I was on my way down and out. I was going to lose and ruin everything, for what? For the very things I said that I wouldn't dare do. I was about to. I have to be crazy as hell. I must have lost my mind. Ya!, pretty much, wow! The sad thing is, Oh God, I want to do it. I want to do all those things, because that is what I know now I understand why it is so important that we bring up our children in the way like you said. It is in moments like these that we turn to you. So many of us you know. We knock it, and we shouldn't. I don't even know how to do this.

I can't share it with Raymond, because I don't trust him. Lord, even though I'm sharing it with you, and I know that you know there's a part of me, that flesh that wants someone to talk too, confine in, to be held, to be loved and told that no matter what. But at the same time I don't want to be like the children of Israel. They wanted to have a King. You kept telling them that they didn't need a King; you were all that they needed. Now I find myself in the same place wanting something else when you should be enough.

The next three or four days were good, Mama, my sister and I spending time together. So I had something other than my problems to think about. When my sister first left the hospital, she stayed with a friend. Because of what was happening in my home, she thought it would be best, but she later realized that was a bad decision. So I made sure that Raymond did not mine her being here, before I told Her it would be okay.

I need the Lord to save me, because no one knows what I do and I'm so glad that my sister was here with me. Even though she is here to recover from her surgery some kind of way her being here was helping me. I think that in the back of my mind, that her being here. Would not have to many episodes of breaking down or out. I soon realized that when it came to pain, hurt, and an overwhelming sense of loss, it does not matter who is around. Help me not to be a fool Lord. Help me not; just help me do what I need to do, because that is the only way. I'm going down if you don't, I'm going to fall, and Lord I don't want to fall.

There is nothing hidden from you. Please, please help me God I need you, I need you so badly. Please God don't let me go, please don't let me go. (She breaks down) I need you Father. I need you to remove this that is in me. I need you Lord to remove those things which are not good for me away, because I don't have the strength to do it. Don't let me fall; don't let me become an open shame please, Oh Jesus. Thank you, Oh Lord thank you. Oh God I praise your holy name, Jesus. Glory be to your name Jesus. Oh God I praise you. I lift you up Father, and I thank you Jesus. My mind is messed up, and I need you to help me straightened it up.

I make my way from the floor onto the bed, finding myself having more and more of these broken moments with Jesus. When the pain of it all seems to be unbearable I find my heart and spirit crushed, and the only person that I will call is the name of Jesus. Even when I find myself feeling indifferent to him I still know that he is the source of strength and help for me. Now how is that for getting something twisted? I felt the need to write Raymond a letter and so I did.

Dear Raymond,

I remember when you used to have to touch me. It made me feel so loved by you. Our love making had passion to it. Then all things changed and I never thought that other women were getting the love that you used to give me. If I did not start then there would be no sex, and even then at times you would make a point to say you were tried or sleepy. Then there were times you would turn your back to me, and when I would touch you, you would pull away. I felt rejected by you. There was no more of a need to satisfy me. You went as far to say that I better learn how to get mine. It was so much easier to deal with when I thought that we were going through what happens in marriages, but when you find that other women were beating your time, and that it was that you loved me, but you just didn't want me, that's a whole new low. In my mind I was not nor am I now enough for you, and you will hurt me deeply all over again. We don't talk, not really. We make small talk, because you love talking to other women more. It never took hours or days to talk, but you shut down and you won't open up. I'm sorry that I have made your life a living hell. That was never my intent. You may love me, but I don't think that you are happy with me. I think that you are happy with someone else and if you really want to be with them then I want you to go and be happy. I love you and I always will. Love like what I feel for you doesn't go anywhere. You won't have to worry about running into me. You can just get on with your life and truly be happy. I love you just that much.

Love,
Kathy

What a beautiful Monday morning and I'm out taking my walk, but I want to talk about last night. When we got into bed Raymond kissed me, and I let him because he started having a problem with the way that I kiss, and that told me that he learned to kiss another woman differently and he likes the way he kissed her. He no longer likes the way I kissed. We really just stopped kissing a lot. That hurt because I can't help knowing that it is because of another woman. He's done or is doing this thing and I'm trying to move pass it, and I'm trying to figure out how I am going to move pass something when he keeps bringing it into my life. He rubs and touches me ways that he hadn't touched me in so long, until I had forgotten that he even knew how to do those things.

He went down and up my body and he touched spots that he had never attempted to touch before, in over ten years and that's a long time not to even attempt to touch my body. Areas that are sensitive and to cause me to have organisms that make me draw up make my body shake uncontrollably, but he did those things. When he did those things it brought more things back to mind. He made love to me. He got on his knees and he made love to me, and it was good. God it was good. It was good, yet it was so painful. It was so really painful because that's when I really knew that he had not been taking any effort nor time with me, and that he was giving all his time and effort to those other women. He cared more about being passionate and making love with them than he did with me. He told me that he didn't make love, he fucked, so what was he saying? Was he fucking me and making love to them?

That's a painful thing to deal with or even be told to realize that not only were they beating your time, but that they replaced me. They had really replaced me and all I was to him was Old Yellow, faithful to the end. I was his maid, a servant and nothing else. I wasn't his wife, friend, lover or anything else. I stopped being anything to him. I stopped being everything to him.

"Oh God, that's a hard pill to swallow." It's hard to live with let alone accept. But it's just another long list of things that I have to deal with, and I just don't know how to deal with it. I don't know how well I'm going to deal with it. I just know I will have to come to terms with. I may continue to hug and kiss on him, but I don't think I will take the lead with him again. It will have to be for him to make love to me. He will have to want it to take place. I don't think he wanted to do it last night, I think that he did it because I wrote him that letter. He's not doing these things because he wants to. If he really felt that way then he never would have stopped doing those things. He was fine with the way his life was. He was busy giving his love to other women like Jonita, Wanda Reed King, Khymesha Davis her mother, Cassandra Davis, and Candice, I don't know how many others there were.

Making it rain, making it rain, so he says. Ya he can do all those things. He can make a woman's body respond, but I don't think he will ever make my heart rain again. I'm not saying that I don't love him. I'm not saying that I don't want him. I'm just saying that I don't need him. I want him and love him. I wish our life could be wonderful together, but every day or every time something like that happens, like last night it only confirms to me all those things I thought and those things I see. The things that I feel, that they were true and still true. He can tell me all he wants, but he is actually showing me is how much he doesn't care. We say oh I'm going to change or I will do this, but we never think of the negative aspect of what we have or have not done, and it will never occur to him if I don't point it out. What he really is doing is showing me just how much he didn't care or love me.

All the things that he is now trying to do, he never would have stopped doing them. Even when he stopped the passion, or I couldn't get my hair done, cause he was giving his money to the other women. Even when we didn't know how the bills would get paid, my love for him never slacked. It never grew weary or cold. It never became indifferent. My love for him stayed and it held fast. It was true to what it believed, to what it felt. It was true to the cause, but not his love, not his because he never had it, and I doubt very much that he has it now, because it's not something that you can pretend. It's something that you have to live, it's something that you have to breathe. It's something you have to know in your knowing and I don't think that he knows any of those things. I don't think that he is even aware of those things. It's okay; it's going to have to because there is nothing that I can do about it. I can't change him. I can't make him something that I want him to be. If he's not that man then he's not that man. He cuts it on and off when it suits him, when it is to his advantage so I'll just have to live with it until God tells me different. I looked at him and know the truth, and I see the truth. I have to worry about maintaining my Godly flow so that I am alright. I don't want to get caught up in him ever again because he has torn me down, and I mean the hell down. He broke me down and I don't ever want to be broken down like that ever again. I don't ever want to be broken and torn like that by nobody ever again and at least of all him. The only way for that to happen is there will have to be a place in my heart that no one can come, not even him.

I always thought married people were supposed to be united, but we are not, at least that is not the way Raymond sees it. We can be together, but not united. I'm learning just how much not to love a man. He talked about me like a dog to those women. He says he didn't, but he did and they were all okay with that, because it justified what he did and when he did it. That's why he always did it when he got upset, when things in our life didn't go well, or he blamed me for something, because it made it easier for him to do what he was about to do. It gave him an excuse, a reason, so that he would be able to look into the mirror and not have himself to blame. He blamed me for it, so he did what he did as a way of punishing me. He punished me, and he did a good job at it, like when he told his niece she needed a damn wake-up call. It's about time, her ass need to wake up. I would like to know wake-up from what Raymond?

Wake-up from the lie I was living, that our marriage wasn't shit and it didn't mean a damn thing to you? That our marriage was dust to dust and ashes to ashes. That this marriage won't ever be what I thought it was. I know because it was never shit from the beginning. I don't want it to be that way, but I can't afford to be a fool and think that it won't. I've lived a lie the whole marriage and now I have to do what I need to do for me. I need to focus on me and my life. I need to build a life that I can have with or without him in it. I need to do what I need to do to make my life better for me. I wish our love making could be like that all the time, but I am only too aware of how bad our marriage is, and I know that it will remain that way because Raymond prefers to go after other women than to satisfy the one that he has at home.

One day I will be able to look back at this and see where this has pushed me, to the place that I need to go. I will be able to see that it only made me stronger than I had ever been. I pray only that it is with you that I have gained much strength. It is with you Lord and not by myself. I pray that with you Lord I do survive this, cause I cannot put any hope in him and survive. He can flip the script on me at anytime. That's life. Now he keeps up with my body and how I'm losing weight. He is keeping up with the way that I'm getting in shape. I don't want him to desire me because I'm losing weight and getting into shape. He didn't desire me when I was big so don't start now that I'm getting small. That is why, I'm doing what I'm doing for me. I will be shapely and my body will look really nice, and I will feel good about myself. I know that men will look at me and women too and I know the attention will stroke my ego, but the one thing I must remember in that is God is my only source of help. He is the only one to give me and help me with what I need. I'm human and I will want all those things. I know that I am and I'm going to act as if I'm not, because I have not arrived. With the help of God, Jesus, and the Holy Ghost I'll make it.

Dear Raymond,

I want to be happy with you, but like I said this morning, it's more fear than anything. I know you say that you want a life with me, but for everyday that you keep doors open and can't shut them makes that fear much greater. I will never be able to turn a blind eye, because to do that would be to keep myself open to much pain. Everyday I wonder will they call or text today. Will you lie again about where you are going, just so you can be with and see them? Even though I love you, my love for you can't keep me from the pain that you bring when you do that.

When you had sex with me on the other night it was wonderful, and I had truly forgotten what it could be like between us. It made me feel that all I was thinking was true. You told me that you could not get up on your knees and it was always some excuse, but for me it was that you were too busy making love to them and just fucking me. Now I don't know how to deal with that. It makes me sad and my heart aches. I'm afraid to look forward to that with you on a regular basis. I don't want to get used to something that may stop again, so while you are trying to do what you can to make our marriage work, I just want you to know how I am feeling about things. I am not trying to make it hard or not work with you, but I must not be crazy to think that this could not happen again, and that is a fear that I must deal with. Though you say that what I think is wrong nevertheless it is what I think and feel, and if this had been done to anyone else they probably would think some of the same things.

Even though I wrote the letter to Raymond, I never did give it to him to read, because I think it was more for me to stay focus, than for him to know what I was feeling about last night.

We were supposed to go to the movie, but as usual, we did not go because he was tired and he had to go back to the office and finish up paperwork. It burns me up, because those same thoughts keep coming back. I don't understand why he is so tired now, but when he was making time to see and screw other women he had all the energy in the world. Now that he has stopped so he says, but his energy level for me has not gotten any better. When he returned home and came to bed, I felt there was no need to sit up, since we were not going anywhere.

Raymond asked me how I felt about him doing ministry. I said,

"I don't have a problem with that. I know that is something you were going to have to do." I don't understand why God was doing it now because he had messed up and I was messing up. I don't understand God's logic or his timing of it all. So I said, "How do you feel?"

Raymond said that he was okay with it, because he knew from the time he was a teenager the call that God placed on his life.

Then I looked at this asshole and wondered why the hell he went and did some shit like that. He caused me to go through what I'm going through. There are demons that we all have. I will say it time and time again. If we do not deal with them, they will deal with us. Some things we can just walk away from until something happens and we go back to our vomit. Getting high was my pass time. I always felt better after smoking a joint. So not only did I drink, but I also got high. I was high every day, all day. That was the only way I could cope with anything, or the only way I wanted to cope. It was very easy to do.

Raymond was at work and I didn't have to worry about him slipping up on me. He was too busy with those women still. So he couldn't give our marriage or me the attention that was needed. So the getting high worked for me. I could look at him and lie in the same bed with him, because being high made it easy for me. It helped to dull my senses, and at the same time it gave me courage to do things. Now I had fallen by the way side, and now I have to get myself together, God told me I have to do what I have to do to get myself together. It's either me or it? I will either live for him and do what I'm supposed to do or, I'm going to die. Why didn't you do this to Raymond when he was out there messing our life up? I don't get why you are doing this to me now. Now you allow this stuff to happen, now that we are torn up, from the floor up. The bad thing about this is that what I'm doing is not hurting anyone but me. I don't want to stop doing it. Nobody has to be involved in what I'm doing. I can be all by myself and do what I do. But I can't, I have to stop, if I don't then I lose everything. Now the crazy thing about that is I feel as if I have already lost everything. In fact I feel as if I never had anything because it was all based on a lie. I will lose my life and my soul and that is something I don't want to lose. So I'm angry, upset, and aggravated and I don't understand why God could not have done something other than this, right here. I don't get it. I really don't.

Okay I did it. I got rid of everything, but one. I'm going to do this one and then I'm on my own. I know now why God wanted me to stop, because all it did was dull the pain. That way I didn't have to deal with the pain. I was just letting it go by, just letting time that I didn't have go by. I hoped that eventually it would just go away, but God didn't want that. He wanted me to depend completely and totally on him. He wanted to heal me. He was taking too long for me to get over the pain, the thoughts. He's just taking too long. These things always turn into years and years of suffing. Years and years of going through this pain and I just don't want to do it anymore. I guess I wouldn't feel so bad, but I just feel like our marriage has been a lie from the beginning. I can't help but feel this way. This "nigger" was running a game on me, from the very beginning, and I don't know how to deal with that. I don't know what to do with it. I don't know how to. I know I needed to stop, but it really doesn't matter because I feel as if I have already lost everything. Now I feel as though I never really had anything, and it's not to say that he didn't do things because I can't take anything from him. But he doesn't realize what he did. And now I'm supposed to try and figure out how to make it work. I don't know how to do it. I can never seem to have these thought without the tears coming. Oh God it hurt so bad, I don't want to feel the pain anymore. I can't keep doing this. I don't know how things are going to turn out. I don't know what's going to happen to us, to him, or to me. All I do know is that I'm just tired of hurting and I'm tried of being hurt. Loving someone should never hurt like this, not to the point that you wish that you never did. Now all I can do is suck it up and suffer through it the best I can. That's the only way to deal with it. Again, I need to write. This time, not a letter to Raymond. Instead, I need a poem for me:

> When I take my hand and rub down the side
>   of your face
> When my finger tips trace the outline of your
>   mustache
> Or I hold your head between my hands
> Placing my lips against your lips
> Can you feel the power of my love for you
>
> When I take my hand and rub the top of
>   your head
> Working my way down your back, pulling
>   your chest close to mine
> Feeling the warmth and sensation it creates
> Can you feel the power of my love for you

When I take my legs and intertwine them
    with yours
Or I take my feet and rub up and down your
    body
When we join our bodies together as one
Can you feel the power of my love for you

I wonder can you feel with each touch
I wonder can you feel with each stroke
I wonder can you feel with each taste
Can you feel what I'm giving
When I give the power of my love for you.